SKELETON PASS

Prospecting for gold in the mountains, Pan Warlow discovers a bonanza — but does not live to enjoy his good fortune. Accidentally blowing himself up, he brings about a cataclysmic avalanche. Now he lies buried beneath a pile of rocks in Skeleton Pass — alongside $200,000 worth of gold belonging to wealthy banker Lanning Mackenzie. Lanning's daughter Flora is determined to find the treasure, aided by her Aunt Belinda, Dick Crespin and Black Moon. But she is in danger from the notorious outlaw Loupe Vanquera . . .

JOHN RUSSELL FEARN

SKELETON PASS

Complete and Unabridged

LINFORD
Leicester

First published in Great Britain in 1950

First Linford Edition
published 2016

*A catalogue record for this book is available
from the British Library.*

ISBN 978–1–4448–2860–3

Published by
F. A. Thorpe (Publishing)
Anstey, Leicestershire

Set by Words & Graphics Ltd.
Anstey, Leicestershire
Printed and bound in Great Britain by
T. J. International Ltd., Padstow, Cornwall

This book is printed on acid-free paper

1

A thin plume of dust, thirty miles out from Mowry City, in New Mexico, was the only visible disturbance in the shimmering wilderness. It marked the progress of a solitary stagecoach, rattling its way across the desert wastes, bound for Winslow in Arizona, a gruelling drive of some three hundred miles, a rugged journey which would lead through the Mongolian Mountains where, it was planned, a halt would be made for the night.

The occupants of the stagecoach's driving seat could not have been more assorted. There was Bill Himmel, the veteran driver, who knew every reaction of the sweating team his gnarled hands controlled; whilst on his right sat the inscrutable figure of Jake Carlow. Jake was six-foot-six, incredibly bony, with a face like tanned oxhide. His jaws moved with the ceaseless energy of a cow over the quid of tobacco he was chewing. He spoke in monosyllables, punctuating them with streams of tobacco juice directed at the trail. He had made the hard trip many a time before. It was his job to see that the gold consignment from Mackenzie Bank in Mowry City reached Winslow safely.

To Bill Himmel's left was a youngster of perhaps eight years of age, his eyes wide in childish interest as he surveyed the arid landscape or looked in eager silence at the rifle beside Jake Carlow's bony knee. The boy had refused to sit with his mother inside the coach, and she, knowing he was safe enough with the hard-bitten guys on the box, had not unduly pressed the matter. The boy wanted to know what was going on around him. Not for a moment would he admit that the seat was uncomfortable or that the smell of the hot horseflesh nauseated him. He wanted one day to be a coach driver himself and handle six-guns like his pop — Jed

Oakes, a US marshal.

'I reckon we'll be lucky, Jake, if we make the Mongolians by sundown,' Bill Himmel said presently, squinting into the arid blaze of the morning. 'These durned cayuses ain't movin' as fast as they oughta. The heat, I reckon.'

'Yeah.' Jake spat casually at a manzanita thicket as the stage passed it.

'Won't take us all that time, Mister Himmel,' the boy piped up. 'I can see the Mongo mountains from here.'

'Mebbe y'can, son,' Bill Himmel growled, 'but distances out here is mighty deceivin' — mighty deceivin'. All yuh can see is the top uv them mountains. That means it'll be plenty close ter sundown afore we gits to 'em. We ain't going straight there, remember. The trail curves, an' I guess we haveta stop fur a rest now an' agin. These cayuses ain't machines.'

'Mister Himmel, is it true there's gold in those mountains?' the boy demanded excitedly. 'My dad says he's heard of it.'

'Might be,' Himmel answered, musing. 'But I guess no critter has ever found any yet.'

★ ★ ★

Almost exactly at that same moment old 'Pan' Warlow, a grizzled prospector, was wondering about gold, too. He was following a lonely trail through the Mongolian Range. He had approached it from the Puerco River area and, having all the time in the world, was in no particular hurry. In fact Pan Warlow was not just *wondering* about gold: he was *sure* there was some. At one point in the Mongos the yellow stuff was there for the picking up. He had heard it from a fellow prospector who had already struck it rich in this region.

So Pan Warlow, grizzled and cheerful, humming a ditty to himself, rode his little pinto in and out of the mountain passes, through the glades and woodland hearts, up acclivities and down slopes, finally reaching the spot he wanted as the sun was commencing to wester.

Just at this point he was high on a rimrock, overlooking a valley trail fifty feet below. Technically, he was directly above Skeleton Pass, the main way through the range from New Mexico to Arizona.

'Guess this is it, Bullseye,' he murmured to the pinto, and got down stiffly from the saddle. 'I reckon you an' me is entitled to a rest an' a bite to eat, fella, before we git busy. Huh?'

The pinto nodded its eager little head vigorously, so Pan spent a moment or two arranging its water and fodder. This done, he opened out his own provisions, disposed of them, and then sat for awhile in the cool of the evening surveying the rugged scenery. Finally he tugged a creased, roughly made map from his shirt pocket and studied it carefully, comparing it with the landmarks around him.

'Yeah, this is it,' he confided to the pinto. 'Yonder sheer wall, fella, is the place we want, an' just as we figured, there ain't no way of gittin' in 'cept by blastin'. So th' sooner we start th' better.'

He struggled to his feet, stretched himself, then went over to the bedroll on the saddle-bag. From it he took several sticks of dynamite, together with fuse wound about them. Leaving the pinto hobbled to a rock spur Pan started to inspect the crevices in the cliff face.

'Do mighty well,' Pan murmured, reflecting. 'Reckon I oughta be able to git beyond this barrier when this lot's blown away . . . ' and he began to insert the dynamite sticks carefully.

The mountains hid from his vision an approaching stagecoach. Aboard its driving seat there still sat Bill Himmel, Jake, and the tired youngster, whilst within the conveyance the boy's mother rocked and bounced painfully and tried to smile at the discomfort of the journey.

'Wasn't fur wrong in me reckonings,'

Bill Himmel said, as Skeleton Pass came into view. 'Not fur from sunset, just like I sed. Once we're through the Pass I guess we'd better stop fur the night. Cayuses need it, an' I'm durned sure we do.'

'Yeah.' Jake sent forth a brown stream into the whirling dust.

'Giup!' Bill Himmel urged, flicking the whip as the horses laboured on the rise to Skeleton Pass. 'Over this slope, yuh jiggers, then yuh can take it easy fur a bit — '

The harnesses jingled; the shafts creaked. The hard wheels pounded into the endless dust and baked earth. The opening to Skeleton Pass grew larger and larger.

As the Pass was entered the boy looked about him in fascination, discovering for the first time how the place had got its name. In various directions, at the side of the trail and up in the rocks, lay white bones. Some of them had belonged to cattle; others to humans, probably prospectors who had lost their way in the torrid wastes many years before and had died before reaching sanctuary.

Jake looked dourly at a skull grinning a few yards away. The clouds of dust belched into the evening light — Then the world came to an end.

Suddenly there was an explosion of shattering violence. Himmel looked up sharply, his tanned face hard in alarm. Jake Carlow spat, and then stared, fascinated. The boy held on to the seat rail and swallowed once.

It looked from where they were seated as though the entire mountain face on their left had lifted forward. With a growing rumble hundreds of tons of basic granite and limestone got on the move and came thundering down the lofty slopes amidst clouds of dust and dispersing smoke.

The noise grew. A cataclysm had resulted from Pan Warlow's dynamite widening an already eroded fissure.

'Sweet sufferin' hell!' Himmel gasped hoarsely, and lashed the horses with frantic violence.

They jolted forward, straining at the shafts, but it was utterly impossible for them to get clear in time. The rocks came flying downwards, thicker — and thicker still. The coach flew sideways as a mighty rock cannoned straight into it, instantly knocking the three from the box and crushing the young woman inside.

Overturned, the coach was buried in a matter of seconds as the sliding mountain face still poured and pounded upon it. Far up the slope where the disturbance had commenced Pan Warlow and his pinto had ceased to be.

In ten minutes there was only dust, drifting away into the gathering darkness.

*　*　*

The non-arrival of the stage at Winslow set the sheriff of that town on a search, complete with deputies and posse. At

Skeleton Pass he was joined by the sheriff from Mowry City, together with his posse, deputies, and Lanning Mackenzie from the Mackenzie Bank.

In silence the group of men sat on their restive horses, surveying the crumbled ruin which had once been a pass. Now it was a wilderness of rock and earth.

'Well, I reckon it's pretty clear what happened,' the Winslow sheriff said finally, cuffing up his hat on to his forehead. 'There's bin a landslide or somethin' an' that stage musta just bin goin' through when it happened. Ain't the first time there's bin a landfall around these parts.'

'That's the way it looks,' Mackenzie agreed soberly; then he looked up at the heights. 'And unless I'm crazy there'll be more landslides, yet. Just take a look at those rocks up there.'

Those around him followed his gaze. The signs were ominous. Enormous boulders were perched edgewise, held back from rolling by the smaller stones in front of them; but the instant those lesser rocks gave way, either from the action of wind or rain, several more hundreds of tons of rock would come down. There might even be a day, and before very long, when the pass as such would cease to exist. It would merely become a dip in the mountain range.

'I guess there ain't anything we can do here, Mr Mackenzie,' the Mowry City sheriff said at last. 'If we start to dig fur that coach the rest of that stuff's goin' to come down and kill the lot uv us. Even as it is there must be a mile area of rock around here and we've no guide as to where the stage might be buried. I reckon it's just one of those things. Four lives lost and the gold gone. Later, mebbe, when things are safer, we can make an attempt to dig down.'

Mackenzie did not say anything. He was thinking of the lost gold more than the lives of the people of whom he had known nothing. But when he saw the adamancy in the faces of both the

11

sheriffs he knew he had to accept the inevitable.

'Yes, I suppose that's it.' He gave a sigh. 'We'd better get on the move.'

2

Lanning Mackenzie was a humane man. Though he could not help smarting under the loss of his gold he did find time to communicate with the relatives of those lost in the stagecoach disaster, and express his condolences. After this he had to turn his mind to deciding how to make good a deficit of some 200,000 dollars in gold. Not that it was his own personal fortune, but it had to be made good if the bank he owned was to survive.

He managed it — but it took him ten gruelling years and the good faith of his customers. Once this debt was cleared he had the way open to provide for himself and his wife, and adolescent daughter. He prospered, as an honest man should, and in fifteen years from the time of the stagecoach tragedy he was able to retire to his Lazy-G ranch.

Yet even this had its tinge of bitterness for he had no wife with whom to enjoy the leisure years. Pneumonia had taken her from him six months before.

'It's queer sometimes the way fate keeps on bludgeoning us, Flora,' he mused, as he sat one evening on the ranch-house porch with his daughter beside him. 'I guess it's been like that all through my life. First I lost the gold; then I lost your dear mother . . . God be praised I still have you.'

Flora smiled up at him. She was now twenty-two, dark-haired and starry-eyed, with an interesting rather than pretty face. She sat on the low stool beside the wicker chair, her slim brown arms clasped about her knees.

'And you'll have me for a long time to come, dad,' she responded, after thinking for a moment. 'I owe it to you. You have worked like a slave for me — and mum whilst she was alive. Education — and everything.'

'To what end?' her father asked, shrugging. 'You've come back to the

14

Lazy-G and put the brakes on.'

'Oh, I don't know. Somebody has to look after you; and old mother Gordon can't do everything, can she?'

Mackenzie was silent for a moment, tugging at his pipe; then he said:

'I'm hoping, Flora, that some young rancher may turn up somewhere one day and discover that there are other things in this part of the world besides desert and flowers and cattle. You are young and full of life. You ought to be partnered, I guess, same as your mother was at your age.'

Silence. The calm of the evening. At a distant point of the spread the boys of the Lazy-G outfit were busy with the foreman bedding the cattle for the night.

'Y'know, Flora, I still keep thinking about that gold,' Mackenzie said at length. 'Though fifteen years have gone by since it got buried in the rocks, I suppose it must still be there. I've ridden out to the point from time to time and it looks to me as though all the rock falls there are going to be have long since happened. The thought of two hundred thousand dollars lying there unrecovered is pretty galling to me — being of a banking frame of mind. I don't need the money, sure, but only a fool ignores a fortune because he doesn't want the trouble of getting at it.'

'Which means what?' Flora asked, puzzled.

'I've been thinking a lot about trying to recover the stuff. As near as I can tell it's under about a hundred and fifty feet of rock. I've approached several people who might have undertaken the digging, but they all swear it's too dangerous in case more rock falls. I don't believe it ever will, myself. If I wasn't getting so ancient I'd start digging tomorrow!'

'And if you entrust the job to anyone else almost anything can happen,' Flora said moodily. 'To ask anybody around here to start digging for two hundred thousand in gold and not snatch any of it would be like asking for the moon. I know some of them are honest, but most of them are not. I think you'd better let it stay where it is and forget it. In fact, it wouldn't surprise me if some footloose wanderer hasn't already found it and taken it.'

Her father nodded regretfully and knocked the ashes from his pipe. Then he paused in mid-action and looked along the trail which led past the ranch gates. In the long beams of the evening sun two horsemen were approaching at a leisurely pace, both their animals loaded to capacity with bedrolls and equipment.

'Not often anybody passes here,' Flora remarked in surprise. 'Wonder where they're headed?'

Her father did not answer. With the girl he continued to watch as the men came nearer. It revealed that one was a broad-shouldered young man in a travel-stained shirt and riding pants, a Stetson cuffed up on his forehead. The other was similarly dressed, but had the lank black hair and inscrutable hatchet features of a North American Indian.

At the gate of the yard of the Lazy-G the riders stopped. The young man in the Stetson dismounted and came across the yard with easy strides. He was tall, Flora noticed, and apparently in his late twenties. He carried a .45 at one hip and his hands were brown and muscular. Then her gaze moved to his face. It was lean-jawed, bronzed with the open air, bright blue eyes contrasting sharply against it. From under the pushed-up hat unruly black curls poked.

'Evening, folks,' he greeted, as he arrived at the porch steps — and on the bottom one he paused, his hand gripping the rail-knob.

'Howdy, young man,' Mackenzie acknowledged. 'Something we can do for you?'

'I guess there is, yes. Black Moon and I are looking for the Sloping-Z. Should be around here somewheres.'

'Black Moon?' Flora questioned.

'Would that be that Indian companion of yours?'

'That's right. He's my servant and handyman. I saved his life a few years back and he's stuck beside me ever since. If he looks fierce that's only because it's natural to him. I reckon he wouldn't hurt anybody, unless he felt it was justified.'

Flora's eyes strayed to the redskin in the dying light, then back to the young man. Her father's wicker chair creaked as he got to his feet.

'Come up on the porch here, young fella. Mebbe you'd like a drink? And Black Moon too?'

'Well, that's mighty nice of you, sir, but I don't want to be a nuisance.'

'Just plain hospitality, son, that's all. Flora, fix a drink for our friends, will you?'

She nodded and got up quickly from the stool, then vanished into the ranch-house. The young stranger signalled to his Indian companion and after a moment or two Black Moon came across the yard, moving with the silent stealth natural to his race. When he had come up on to the porch he gave the Indian sign of greeting but said no word.

Flora returned with the drinks in a moment or two and set them down on the little table nearby; then she contented herself with watching the bronzed young stranger as he drank deeply. To the Indian she paid no atention, despite the fact that his dark, unfathomable eyes were fixed upon her.

'So you're looking for the Sloping-Z?' Mackenzie asked at length. 'I guess it's about twelve miles to the north of here, straight down the trail. Dirk Crespin's spread — or at least it usta be. He died a few weeks back, so if you're thinking you'll meet him you . . . '

'I wasn't thinking that.' The young man's voice was serious as he interrupted. 'I'm Richard Crespin, Dirk's younger brother. Dirk got himself gored by a bull a few weeks ago and died from the effects. Just before that happened he managed to get in touch with me and handed over his entire spread and outfit into my care. So here I am to take over — with Black Moon to help . . . Incidentally, did Black Moon greet you properly?'

'Indian fashion, yes,' Mackenzie answered, smiling.

'He's a bit above the average Indian. He can read and write English — which makes him pretty civilized. Eh, Moony?'

'Black Moon no draw notice to himself when Mr Dick speak,' the Indian commented, in his bass voice.

'Very nice,' Flora approved.

Dick glanced at her and smiled. 'So the Sloping-Z is twelve miles north?' he asked, glancing quickly at Mackenzie again. 'We'd best be on our way, then — and thanks for the information and the drink, Mr — er — '

'Mackenzie,' Mackenzie said. 'I'm Lanning Mackenzie, retired banker, and this is my daughter, Flora.'

'Been nice meeting you both,' Dick

21

said. 'Mebbe we'll see more of each other since we're to be neighbours . . . Well, better be on our way. Come on, Moony.'

Both men turned to leave the porch, then Flora gave them pause as she spoke urgently:

'Just a minute, Mr Crespin! I don't think my father has been particularly explicit in saying the Sloping-Z is twelve miles to the north. It is, of course, but it isn't as easy as all that. The night's coming, and you might easily lose your way.'

'Not with Black Moon. He can follow a trail anywheres.'

'I think,' Flora said, 'it might be better if I showed you the right direction. I know it backwards.'

Her father looked at her blankly for a moment, but did not pass any comment. When she turned to glance at him her eyes seemed brighter than usual.

'Don't you think I'm right, dad?' she questioned eagerly.

'Up to you, Flora. Come to think of it, it is a tricky way to follow.'

Flora did not need any further incentive. She hurried down the steps from the porch and went round to the stables at the rear of the ranch-house. In a moment or two she had returned, leading a pinto and carrying his saddle.

'Get him ready for me, Mr Crespin, whilst I change,' she requested, and he nodded promptly.

Mackenzie, within earshot, grinned to himself. He returned to his wicker chair, lighted his pipe, and then sat watching whilst Dick Crespin buckled on the saddle and then stood waiting with Black Moon beside him. Flora came into view again presently, in silk shirt, leather jacket and riding trousers. She swung easily into the saddle and Dick Crespin and the Indian kept up with her as she trotted the pinto across the yard.

The twilight was dissolving into night when all three started off along the trail. By the time they had covered the first mile the darkness had arrived with its myriads of brightly glittering stars.

'It's very kind of you to take all this trouble on my behalf, Miss Mackenzie,' Dick said at length, as she rode beside him.

'Oh, just being neighbourly — as my father would say,' she answered, laughing. 'When you're not familiar with the district it isn't easy to find your way around . . . Where exactly do you hail from, Mr Crespin?'

'Telluride, Colorado. I had a small spread and trading post there. Didn't do so badly. But I think I can make a good deal more out of the Sloping-Z, so I packed everything up and came riding over. We've been on the journey for quite a few days. No easy trip, believe me.'

'I can imagine,' Flora responded, and for a time rode on in silence again. In fact, the conversation was very limited for the next few miles; then Dick spoke with an air of wonderment.

'Frankly, Miss Mackenzie, I don't see

anything particularly complicated about this trail — nothing, that is, to demand you having to make the trip to the Sloping-Z and back.'

'That was an excuse,' Flora said.

'Excuse? For what?'

'I may be a little old-fashioned, Mr Crespin, but I believe in Providence.'

'Yeah? Well, that isn't old-fashioned. It's the natural thing with anybody, if they're normal.'

'I'm glad to hear you say that. It confirms my opinion of you. I believe, you see, that my father and I have made your acquaintance for a very real reason.'

Since this completely mystified him Dick made no comment at all. Flora studied him but could not determine his expression. Beyond him again she could see the frozen profile of the redskin against the stars as he rode along.

'It concerns gold,' Flora said at length. 'Two hundred thousand dollars' worth of it, to be exact. It's buried under a landslide of fifteen years standing in the Mongolian Range in Arizona. Father can't find anybody he'd trust to dig it out. Somehow, I don't think he need look any further.'

Dick laughed incredulously. 'You're taking a good deal for granted, aren't you? Just why do you imagine I am to be trusted any more than the next man?'

'I just do, that's all. Women can sense those things. I'm convinced you can help us.'

'Well, I will if I can, of course, if only to be neighbourly. What exactly are the facts?'

Flora gave them unhesitatingly, so instinctively did she feel that Dick Crespin was the kind of man to whom she could talk with confidence. By the time she had finished her narration the twelve-mile journey was nearly at its end and in the dawning moon-rise the distant bulk of the Sloping-Z had become vaguely visible.

'From what you say, the rock fall

must be considerable,' Dick Crespin commented at length. 'It might take quite a while to dig down, especially since I don't know where to look. I am not so sure I can afford the time.'

'You won't be expected to do it for nothing,' Flora said. 'My father is already a rich man. With two hundred thousand dollars added he'll be more than generous. I think you'd find the money useful, particularly as you are just starting up in business at the Sloping-Z.'

They had reached the deserted bulk of the Sloping-Z before Dick spoke again. Then he drew his horse to a halt and looked at the girl in the moon-light.

'I appreciate the trust you put in me, Miss Mackenzie. If I wanted, I could go right now to that one-time pass and start searching for myself.'

'If I'd have thought you were the kind of man who'd do that I wouldn't have told you anything.'

'I can't give a snap decision on this.

It depends on how things make out at my ranch here. And something else occurs to me: I take it you would come to the pass also?'

'Naturally.'

'I don't see how you could. You and me — alone there, except for Black Moon. Not quite the thing, is it?'

'For an open-air man you're terribly ethical,' Flora said seriously. 'Anyhow, I have it all worked out. I have a maiden aunt living in Mowry City who'll come along. She's loud-mouthed, tub-thumping, and a terrible nuisance, but at least she'll be a chaperon.'

Dick laughed. 'Against all this opposition I guess I don't stand much chance — and I still want to think it over. I'll ride out to your spread tomorrow and let you know what I can do. How's that?'

'I know you'll help us,' Flora said, shaking the strong hand he held out. 'You walked right into the picture for a definite reason. I'm absolutely sure of that.'

And without giving him opportunity for further words she swung round the head of her pinto and went galloping off into the moonlight. Dick stood looking after her and scratching the back of his neck.

'Good job I'm an honest man, Moony, or she'd certainly land herself in for a lot of trouble!'

'Honest man not make profit for self, Mister Dick,' the Indian answered ambiguously. 'Much money in the pass — more than we ever saw. You dig it up. Get small reward. Black Moon no like.'

'The reward I'll get, Moony, will be the respect and friendship of Miss Mackenzie — and for me, starting up in a new and lonely region, that means a lot. Even more than money.'

The redskin reflected. Flora Mackenzie was of a different race to himself and he could not possibly understand the white man's reaction to her.

'Black Moon think plan no use,' he said finally. 'Much gold not lie untouched for fifteen years. By now

Loupe Vanquera will have taken.'

'The Mexican bandit? I doubt that, Moony. Just because he's a notorious outlaw and a bank robber it doesn't follow that he'd be able to smell out buried gold. In fact, I don't think he'd get the chance. He has to keep on the move, and to work in that one-time pass would keep him in one place too long.'

'Black Moon has spoken,' the Indian responded doggedly, then he turned and began moving towards the ranch.

Dick Crespin kept his word and arrived at the Lazy-G towards noon the following morning. Though Flora was apparently busy attending to the riot of flowers on the porchway, he had the impression that she had been waiting for him. Her surprise at his call of greeting was not particularly convincing.

'Naturally,' she said, smiling brightly as he took off his hat and shook hands, 'you are going to help us?'

'Well, yes, but I . . . '

'Oh, I knew you would! I made all arrangements, even to asking my aunt to come over. You'd better come in and see dad.'

Dick nodded and followed her into the ranch-house living-room. Mackenzie was busily attending to correspondence at the bureau by the window, but he got up quickly enough as the young rancher entered.

'I guess there's little I can say, Mr Crespin,' he exclaimed, as he shook hands. 'Flora seems to have made up her mind about this gold-digging business — and when she does that I just don't count. Takes after me in one thing: she's obstinate.'

'I — er — noticed,' Dick agreed, laughing.

'Seriously, though, can you spare the time?' Mackenzie asked.

'I think so.' Dick sat down as Flora motioned to chairs. 'Since my brother died the foreman of the spread has been handling things, and apparently he can go on doing it indefinitely. I'm taking on this gold-digging job because I think it might benefit me financially.' Dick hesitated. 'I am sorry to bring that aspect into it, Mr Mackenzie, but I have to. I've got to make my way, and this looks like a scheme which will help me do it.'

'No doubt of it,' Mackenzie agreed. 'That gold, when it is found, is my legal property. I stood its loss and paid back the bank depositors from my own profits. I'm willing to make a fifty-fifty deal with the man who can dig it up intact.'

Dick opened his mouth and then shut it again. He started.

'Fifty-fifty!' he ejaculated. 'That's crazy!'

'I thought the terms were pretty generous,' Mackenzie replied.

'They're *too* generous, sir: that's what's the matter! Do you realize that you are promising me one hundred thousand dollars if I can find the gold?'

'Of course I realize it. Don't forget the other side. If I cannot find somebody to dig up the stuff I get nothing; and that is why I'm prepared to split the proceeds. Your share ought to set you up nicely on that spread of yours.'

Whatever hesitation Dick might have had when he arrived, it had all gone now. He got to his feet actively.

'Before I left my spread I gave instructions to Moony for him to pack a horse with all requirements,' he said. 'That means there is nothing to prevent me starting off for the pass right now.'

He glanced at Flora and she smiled. 'Yes, I'm coming too,' she said, interpreting his look. 'I'm waiting for aunt to come over. She'll be here any minute. Otherwise I'm ready — with my pinto loaded with necessities. Aunt will come on her own horse, I expect.'

'She will?' Dick looked surprised. 'I didn't know that middle-aged ladies cavorted about on cayuses in this region.'

'You don't know Aunt Belinda,' Flora said solemnly.

'On my late wife's side,' Mackenzie hurried to explain as though he wished to disavow all relationship with the woman.

Ten minutes later Dick thought he understood why. Aunt Belinda rode into the ranch yard, and the view through the window revealed her as a massive woman in the middle fifties, wearing riding trousers, a check shirt and half-boots. A Mexican-style hat was at an angle on her brown hair and she marched into the ranch with strides which would have done credit to a six-foot cowhand.

'Howdy,' she acknowledged, as she came stalking into the room. 'How in hell are you, Lanning? An' you, Flora? Darned hot again!'

'I'm fine, aunt,' the girl answered promptly. 'This is Mr Crespin from the . . .'

'Dang it, girl, give me the chance t'finish hands with yuh dad first, can't yuh?' Belinda demanded. 'I'll come t'you, mister, when I'm good an' ready.'

Dick stared at her but did not say anything. Flora's pink cheeks went a little pinker and she shifted from one foot to the other; then her aunt swung round and gripped Dick's hand in a bone-cracking clutch.

'So yore the youngster who's runnin' the Slopin'-Z now, huh?' she demanded, her piercing grey eyes searching him from head to foot. 'Mmm — I don't know but what you mightn't make a job of it at that! Plenty of power in them limbs, but yore gettin' flabby on the belly. Check that, son. Won't d'yuh no good out here. Lanning here's gotta belly, an' look how he sits around! To live at all around hereabouts yuh've gotta be cast iron an' whipcord. Savvy?'

'I — I think so, ma'am,' Dick assented, astounded.

'Good enough!' Belinda roared, and banged him violently on the back. Then she tossed up her head and impaled Flora with a challenging eye. 'Well, what's th' delay about? I thought we wus headin' fur Skeleton Pass? — or what's left uv it.'

'That's right, aunt,' Flora agreed hurriedly. 'I have everything ready, and I suppose you have?'

'Me?' Belinda hooted. 'Yore danged tootin'! Every durned thing, includin' my umbrella.'

'But it won't rain!' Dick exclaimed.

'Rain? In Arizony? At this time o'year?' Aunt Belinda bellowed with laughter. 'Shucks, I don't take me umbrella fur rain, son! I use it instead uv a rifle, I reckon yuh can beat the livin' daylights out uv anybody with an umbrella if yuh know how ter use it . . . Well, come on! What in heck are we stymied fur?'

Flora shifted position and glanced at her father. He asked a question mildly:

'When do you expect to be back?'

'Why?' Belinda asked tartly. 'Afeared of th' dark?'

'Oh, don't be so ridiculous, Belinda! I merely wish to . . . '

'Listen!' Belinda interrupted, her jaw projecting. 'Yuh want this gold uv yourn dug up, don't yuh? Yuh don't want it in tiny bits and pieces: yuh want the whole shoot. Okay, then, that ain't th' kind uv job y'can do in five minutes. We'll be back when we're good an' ready . . . Now let's go!'

She gave one fierce glare around her, as though viewing an invisible army, then she led the way on to the porch, the grinning Dick coming up behind her. At the porch rail, the reins looped to it, stood her sorrel, loaded to the limit with necessities. The umbrella could not help but be noticed and Dick gazed at it in fascination. Belinda tugged it from the special leather sheath on the saddle and opened it with a noise like a flapping tent. It was the grandfather of all umbrellas, as large as a beach-umbrella, with an ash shaft and whalebone ribs.

'Yes, sir!' Belinda declared, waving it over her head until Dick began to wonder if she'd perhaps become airborne in the wind blowing across from the plains. 'Any critter who gits in my way sure gets one helluva crack with this.'

She closed it up again emphatically and thrust it back in the scabbard, then she looked at Flora.

'Ready, gal?'

Flora nodded. 'My pinto's at the back, loaded up. I'll join you.'

She turned away and Aunt Belinda swung with practised ease to the saddle of her horse. She eyed Dick as he settled astride his own mount.

'I don't see much sign of anythin' worth havin' on that mount uv yourn,' she said. 'This ain't just a canter, young fella, or hadn't yuh realized that?'

'I'm picking up my stuff along the trail. My spread is nearer Skeleton Pass than here. No use bringing the stuff this far, only to take it all the way back.'

'Logical,' Belinda agreed, nodding vigorously. 'Yuh'll git on, young fella: yuh think things out ahead. I figger yuh've a redskin comin' with yuh?'

'Black Moon. He's my servant as well as my best friend.'

'Good enough: they're a breed that knows the way around if we run into trouble ... Hell's bells, gal,' Belinda broke off, her voice roaring across the yard, 'how much longer are yuh goin' t'be?'

Flora appeared at that moment, astride her pinto, all her needful belongings in the saddle-bag. With a jab of her heels Belinda set her sorrel cantering forward. In a moment or two she, Dick and Flora had reached the trail which ran directly past the yard gates. They swung northwards, the horses galloping briskly.

'Nothin' like this durned country t'keep yuh healthy,' Belinda declared presently, drawing in breath vigorously. 'Take a look round yuh. If yuh don't think it's worth bein' alive fur I reckon yuh'd be better off dead.'

Dick glanced towards Flora and winked. She only smiled seriously, looking half embarrassed by the behaviour of this extraordinary woman to whom she was unavoidably related. Not that there was anything really wrong with Belinda: she just happened to exude energy, power and generosity. She was full of tremendous high spirits and meant everybody near her to be — or else. There was plenty of truth, too, in her statement concerning the environment.

At the moment the New Mexico countryside was at its very best. To left and right of the trail spread the fields of golden brittle-bush, the creamy white of the yuccas upthrusting here and there from the midst. And where the fields of brittle-bush gave way to rich pasture lands there were the yellow and red lichens peeping out from amongst the purple pentstemon. Primrose, anemone, loco-weed — they were all there, filling the warm breeze with a magic and exhilarating perfume. And overhead, to complete the picture, a grosbeak maintained a liquid flow of song.

'There's Moony,' Dick said presently, when the bend of the trail brought them within sight of the Sloping-Z.

The redskin was seated on a gelding at the yard gate, bedrolls and equipment fastened to the saddle's rear. Then it became clear that he had a second, smaller horse beside him, fully loaded with shovels, camping equipment and every necessity.

'This looks like business,' Belinda decided in satisfaction. 'I reckon we oughta be able t'do somethin' with that tackle. How are yuh figgerin' on sleepin'?' she asked, as though the thought had only just struck her.

'I've two tents there,' Dick responded. 'You haven't brought one, have you?'

'Me? Shucks, what would I want with a tent? I sleep under the stars, or nothin' — an' it'd do th' rest uv yuh good t'do the same!'

'Black Moon does,' Dick replied. 'It won't be anything new to him. So I'll take one of the tents and you, Miss Mackenzie, can have the other.'

'Miss Mackenzie?' Belinda repeated blankly. 'Hell, she's gotta first name,

41

ain't she? Use it, durn it! That's what it's fur!'

Dick gave a smile as he caught the girl's nod, then he turned to Black Moon when the Sloping-Z was reached.

'Everything ready, Moony?'

'Black Moon prepare,' the Indian assented, and with an impassive nod to Flora and her aunt, he nudged the two horses forward along the trail.

'Sure is a genooine redskin,' Belinda commented. 'Mute as hell an' tough as they come.'

Hereafter she said very little, giving all her attention to her riding. The journey to the Mongolian Range was no easy one, the trail leading across sheer desert once the pasture lands were left behind. By sundown that evening four blistered travellers had completed some seventy-five miles, and, being amidst a rock outcropping, made their camp for the night.

After the meal they lay under the stars and talked for awhile — or rather Belinda talked and Flora and Dick listened. Black Moon took no part in the proceedings at all. He sat some distance away, inscrutable and silent, his gaze on the starlit expanses.

'I reckon we should make the Mongolian Range by noon tomorrow,' was Belinda's final observation; then she wrapped herself in blankets and promptly went to sleep, her snores just as noisy as her voice had been.

Dick spent a little while making sure that the girl's tent was to her liking, then he bade her goodnight and settled down for a final smoke before turning into his own tent nearby. Presently the tall, dark shadow of Black Moon appeared beside him, and sat down.

'Black Moon scent danger,' the redskin said.

'You and your Indian signs!' Dick laughed. 'Why don't you grow up and become civilized? Danger be damned! I'm no believer in a lot of silly superstition.'

'The stars do not lie,' Black Moon declared stubbornly. 'Black Moon read

43

much danger. We remain on watch —
all time.'

'You mean there'll be danger in
getting the gold?' Dick asked, a little
more seriously.

'Much danger, Mister Dick. The stars
say it may come through white squaw.'

Dick relaxed, hands behind his head.
'Now I know you're crazy! Who could
possibly imagine Flora being dangerous?'

'Black Moon say danger might come
through white squaw.' The redskin was
silent for a while, scanning the heavens.
Then he added briefly: 'Black Moon
sleep.'

Getting to his feet he wandered off to
a shadowy patch nearby where he
evidently intended to spend the night.

3

It was mid-afternoon of the following day when the quartet reached the one-time pass in the Mongolian Range. All that remained of it was the incline leading up to it — that long slope up which, so many years before, Bill Himmel had unwittingly driven the stagecoach to destruction. Otherwise there was nothing but frowning grey walls climbing peak on ledge into the cloudless cobalt of the sky. Arid — desolate — choking dust blowing in the scorching breeze. Half-way up the mountain sides cedar and juniper reached, then died away towards the greater heights. There hung about the whole area an unpleasant suggestion of death and thirst.

'This ain't going to be any holiday,' Dick said at last, drawing the back of his hand over his streaming forehead.

Belinda swung to him in her saddle. 'Yuh knew what yuh wus a-takin' on when yuh started the deal, didn't yuh?' she demanded. 'This ain't no time t'think uv backin' out.'

'I've no intention of doing so!' Dick retorted, irritated by the heat and the woman's intolerable energy.

'All right, then!' She eyed him fixedly. ''Bout time we got a camp pitched, ain't it, and some cover over us? I reckon this heat's enough t'fry yuh blasted brains.'

'But this isn't the exact spot we want,' Flora pointed out, tugging a copy of a map from her shirt pocket. 'This is only the entrance to the pass. The actual place is about a mile and a half further on.'

'Then let's go there,' Belinda decided logically, and kicked the sorrel's sides.

Dick, Flora and Black Moon followed behind her, their mounts moving slowly, all but exhausted by the grilling blaze above them. Flora, shading her eyes, glanced around her at the mountains, then suddenly she gave a start. She drew rein and sat staring at a point high up on the nearer escarpment.

'What's wrong?' Dick asked, hipping round in his saddle to look at her.

'I — I thought I saw somebody.' Flora's voice was uncertain. 'It looked like a cowboy's hat — and a face — right up there where that ledge sticks out.'

Dick looked at the position she indicated but he failed to detect anything. Black Moon looked too, his face and figure as motionless as though he were carved from teak.

'Imagination, I guess,' Dick said finally. 'The heat does things like that to you sometimes.'

'What do you think, Moony?' Flora asked the Indian, and he took his gaze from the escarpment to look at her.

'White squaw quick eyes,' he answered. 'Black Moon think you may be right.'

Aunt Belinda's voice suddenly roared

forth from further up the slope.

'What th' blue Hades is a-keepin' yuh down there? Are we goin' to pitch camp or ain't we?'

Dick glanced about him. 'Better carry on,' he advised. 'If somebody is up there we can investigate later. Anyway, we haven't the exclusive right to use this pass. No reason to suppose somebody means trouble for us.'

'Much gold mean trouble,' Black Moon said briefly; then he started his horse forward again.

Dick and Flora began to follow him, studying the mountain face as they went; but they saw no more signs — or at least Flora did not. Dick was quite convinced that she had been mistaken.

So, gradually, the wearying climb of the incline was completed, then they had before them the gigantic dip in the landscape where the pass had once been. Now it was little more than a rocky depression several miles long, hemmed in on both sides by the mountain heights. Boulders and dust and searing heat. Nowhere a sign of cover; nowhere a green thing — except high up on the mountain faces.

'Sure is like Death Valley,' Belinda commented, leaning on the saddle-horn and surveying. 'Ain't far short uv bein' as hot, neither. Wonder how long it is since anybody passed this way?'

'This trail goes round the mountain now, instead of through it,' Flora said. 'Has done for years. This spot ought to be completely deserted.'

'Oughta be?' Belinda stared at her. 'Dang it, gal, it *is*! Look at it, stretchin' fur as the eye can reach an' endin' over there in somethin' like a depression.'

'That'll be Eagle's Fold,' Flora replied, fully acquainted with the district. 'It's a kind of neighbouring valley. I haven't ever been to it but it's marked on the local maps.'

'There's a mountain stream to the left there,' Dick commented, nodding. 'We might pitch our camp there. As the sun drops we'll get the shade of the mountains.'

In half an hour the animals had all been watered and fed and signs of a camp were taking shape. By this time the sun, too, had moved position, bringing the first long fingers of welcome shade to the valley floor. Flora and Dick, their own unpacking finished, were relaxed full-length amidst the rocks, doing their best to recover from the journey. The redskin and Belinda, however, were still at work sorting out necessities and the tools for digging.

'You might as well have brought a fire-engine with you for a chaperone,' Dick commented presently, propping himself on his elbow and watching Belinda's comings and goings.

'I warned you what she was like.' Flora gave a little smile. 'She's worth two strong men, Dick, and that's something.'

He surveyed the grey, dusty waste for a moment or two.

'Did it ever occur to you that this might take years?' he asked finally.

'We've no place we can pin-point where we can start digging. Just have to take a chance — and it won't be easy.'

'Suppose it *does* take a long time?' Flora asked. 'Does it matter?'

Dick looked at her in surprise. Her dark eyes were very bright, her soft, waving hair blowing in the hot breeze.

'It might matter a lot,' Dick responded. 'After all I have a ranch to run. You are a rich man's daughter with nothing to worry about. I've a living to make.'

'You seem to have forgotten that you get a hundred thousand out of this when you find the gold.'

Dick smiled wryly. 'And you seem to have forgotten that I may *never* find it. In that case it's time lost.'

Flora hesitated, her finger stirring the sandy dust beside her. She looked away as she spoke.

'I suppose you don't find any compensation in being . . . with me?'

Since Dick did not answer she turned to look at him. His eyes were fixed on her, a faint smile pulling the corners of his humorous mouth.

'Things are evidently different here to Colorado,' he said, musing.

'Different? How *different*?'

'Oh, just that in Colorado the men make the advances to the girl, instead of the other way round. You've got me wondering, Flora: is this a gold-hunt or a joy ride?'

Suddenly Flora was on her feet, angrily. 'Just what do you mean by that? You know perfectly well that this is a genuine hunt for gold. You don't think my father would joke about a matter like that, do you?'

'He wouldn't, but you might.' Dick also rose, giving his dry smile. 'I'm making a guess, Flora. You came on this soul-frying trip, not only because you want to help look for gold, but also because you think I'd make a good husband for you. Right?'

Flora stared at him blankly, never having expected such accurate thought-reading.

'Not that I blame you,' Dick grinned. 'You're a girl who must feel mighty lonely — and I get that way myself sometimes. Only I'm sorta funny . . . I like to make the advances myself. Maybe it's hereditary.'

Flora half started to say something, checked herself, and then turned away fiercely.

'Now what?' Dick asked, following her leisurely. 'If I'm right why not admit it? It'd save an awful lot of time.'

'You — you take too much for granted!' Flora retorted over her shoulder.

Dick came to a stop, shrugging, hands in pockets. He stood watching as Flora kept on walking away from the camp, stumbling and tripping over the loose stones. Then he turned as Aunt Belinda came towards him, breathing heavily, her big red face dew-dropped in perspiration.

'What ails the gal?' she asked briefly. 'Ain't she got no more darned sense than march around in this sun without a hat on?'

'She's sore at me,' Dick answered, as Flora's slim figure vanished behind a distant rock spur. 'I guess she as good as told me we ought to marry each other.'

'That so unusual?' Belinda demanded.

'Nope — only she didn't like the way I anticipated her. I guess it's hard to figger women. They turn round on you when you least expect it.'

'That gal's spoiled,' Belinda decided, and spat gracefully into the dust. 'I never did hold with eddication. No siree! Takes th' fire outa yuh. I reckon you've had a fair eddication too, huh?'

'Not bad. My dad was keen on it.'

'Yeah, an' I reckon that's what's made yuh sappy. Otherwise yuh'd grab the gal, put her over yuh knee, an' give her one across the backside. Yuh should kill tantrums before they start. See?'

'You're taking a lot for granted — as Flora would say,' Dick remarked.

'Where's the proof we want to get married?'

'Proof be dad-blamed!' Belinda roared. 'She says she wants to, but yuh have ter be tough about it and throw it back in her face. I reckon you two couldn't do better'n git into double harness. Frum what I've seen uv yuh yuh'd both make pretty good breeders.'

'We're not cattle, Belinda,' Dick reminded her.

'Who sez you ain't? Cattle on two legs. Ain't no difference. Everything breeds around here — cattle, humans, and doggoned flies . . . ' Belinda finished with a yelp and slapped the back of her red neck with the noise of a pistol shot.

Meantime Flora was wandering onwards and trying to decide at the same time why she was doing it. It occurred to her after a while that only pique had started her off: that Dick had even *dared* to guess what she was driving at.

'You're an idiot!' she said, out loud,

wandering onwards amidst the scorching rocks with the diagonal sun blazing down upon her. 'Now it's perhaps going to take weeks of work to recover the ground you've lost. Dick was all ready, and you had to spoil it! Crass, muddle-headed idiot!'

She continued reviling herself for quite a while; then it began to dawn on her that she was in unfamiliar territory. As far as she could tell she had covered perhaps three miles from the base camp and was now surrounded by rock and frowning mountain walls. There was calmness on everything, a loneliness, which was somehow frightening.

She looked about her. She had come well beyond the depression which lay at the end of the pass. She wondered whether or not to go back, then decided that, at present, Dick would only grin at her if she did. Sunset was not due yet so she could still allow a little time before she began the return journey. So she went on walking, presently coming to an upward rise of land. Here she paused and gazed in astonishment into the small valley below her. A town was standing there. Certainly, as far as she knew, it was not marked on any of the local maps.

Thoughts of a mirage chased through her head for a moment, then she decided this could not be the case. No; the evening sun was casting distinct shadows from the huddle of buildings. It was not a particularly large town, and most of it seemed to be in a state of utter disuse. There was the usual main street, and she recognized the outlines of a general stores, a livery stable, a small trading post, a saloon, and a tabernacle with a broken spire. But not a thing moved. There was only the undisturbed dust in the main street, the quietness, and the overpowering blaze of the sun.

Flora was still youthful enough to be interested in the unusual. She forgot all about her intention to return to the camp and instead went down the slope quickly, reaching the end of the town's main street in perhaps twenty minutes. Here she stopped once more and looked about her.

There was no doubt of it now. Nothing lived. The town had apparently not been tenanted for years. The only explanation was that it was a ghost town, one of the many hundreds of makeshift headquarters which had sprung up in the past during the gold-rush days in the Mongolian Mountains. Yet even now, in all its deserted tranquillity, it had a certain fascination for Flora. She began walking slowly, dust burying her feet to the ankles. Then she stopped and gave a start as she distinctly heard a scream.

She was not sure from where it had come — until it was repeated from a nearer point. This time somebody came into view from one of the narrow alleys between the buildings. He appeared to be a youth of perhaps seventeen, roughly attired in a torn shirt and with trousers frayed away at the knees. His legs and feet were bare; his unkempt dark hair flowed wildly.

For a moment or two Flora could do nothing but stare at him in wonderment — then as he came nearer she realized she had been mistaken in his age. He was probably in the early twenties in years, though definitely child-like in his movements. Suddenly catching sight of her the youth came stumbling in her direction. Almost before she could draw away his hands were clawing at her shoulders.

'He's — he's after me — ' he gasped out hoarsely, using a curious stilted English. 'He's going to hit me — '

Flora did her best to push away the clawing hands, but she did not succeed. Apparently the ragged creature regarded her as his one protection and had no intention of letting go. So Flora finally put an arm about his shoulders comfortingly, only to withdraw it quickly as she contacted something wet and sticky.

It took her five seconds to discover that the quivering youth had been flayed ruthlessly across the back. Blood was still seeping through his tattered shirt from the lashes he had received. A glint came into Flora's eyes as her protective instincts were aroused.

'Who did this?' she demanded, but the youth shook his head dully and did not answer. Instead he pointed back with a thin hand whence he had come.

As he did so Flora saw the cause of the trouble. A big, thick-set man, in dirty trousers and shirt, his mane of white hair flowing in the breeze, was advancing steadily. In one hand he held a stockwhip, such as stagecoach drivers had once used. At first he progressed at almost a run, then when he saw Flora, erect and waiting, he slowed down a little. But he still came forward.

Flora held her ground, clutching the boy's arm. Inwardly she was shaking but the set of her jaw did not betray the fact. She eyed the man as he came up. He had fairly good features, but there was a vacant look in his blue eyes as though some violent shock had bereft him of most of his intelligence. When he spoke it was in a thick, coarse voice.

'Reckon yuh'd better let him go, miss.'

'So you can thrash him some more?' Flora demanded. 'Not if I know it! Get away from him!'

The man reflected, his tongue passing slowly round his cracked lips. Flora's free hand stole down to the butt of the .32 she was carrying at her waist — then she suddenly gasped with pain as the vicious tails of the whip lashed out and struck her across the hand. Blood was not drawn but red weals were left.

'Why, you low-down . . . ' Regardless of the smart in her hand she whisked the gun from its holster, but the whip came again and with deadly accuracy flicked the weapon from her grasp. She stood trembling, her free hand still gripping the youth's further shoulder.

'You don't suppose I'm a-takin' orders frum a slip of a gal like you, do yuh?' the man demanded, a glint in his wild-looking eyes. 'Get that kid free afore I really go ter work on yuh . . . Come here, you!' he bawled at the youth, and at the same moment his whip whistled so the thongs cut relentlessly across the youth's back. He gave a cry like a frightened animal, tore free of Flora's grip, then began running blindly.

The man swung to follow him, only to stop in his tracks at the sudden explosion of a gun. He hesitated, dropping his whip and clutching at his breast, then with his face contorted he sagged into the dust and lay still.

Flora twirled about, searching for the one who had fired the shot. After a moment or two she saw him — or rather them. Two men were approaching from behind one of the buildings, both of them tall and well-built, and, as far as it went, not badly dressed. Flora picked up her gun and held it ready, just in case.

As the foremost man came nearer she saw that he was swarthily dark, dressed in close-fitting black riding pants, black shirt, and fancy half-boots. A black sombrero was at an angle on his shining hair.

'I am sorry, *señorita*, if I startled you,' he apologized, pausing perhaps a foot away and doffing his hat. 'I felt it was necessary to remove such scum as this . . . ' He idly kicked the fallen man in the ribs.

'I'm — er — ' Flora hesitated, backing away. Polished though the man's manner was she did not like him; and even less the henchman with the close-set eyes who stood behind him.

'Why so hurried, *señorita*?' the man asked. 'Have I not saved you a good deal of distress? Am I not entitled to a reward?' And he grinned to reveal big white teeth.

'You — you have my thanks,' Flora stammered, 'and that is all I'm prepared to give . . . '

Then she began running, but before she had progressed a few yards the big fellow had come round in front of her.

Before she could realize what he intended she was crushed into his arms and found herself squirming under a kiss.

'There!' he said, grinning as he released her. 'Loupe Vanquera never asks anything more of a lady . . . '

His words stopped dead as Flora delivered a stinging slap across his face. Then her gun came up sharply.

'Out of my way!' she ordered, her cheeks red with anger.

Vanquera grinned. Quickly as a striking snake he shot out his hand and snatched the gun for himself. Then he surveyed the girl from head to foot as she looked helplessly about her.

'You have not seen me before, señorita, but I have seen you,' he murmured. 'And I liked what I saw. In fact I liked it so much I decided to keep a watch on where you went. Just as well I did. Crazy Bill might have killed you — just as he has almost killed that kid.'

'Crazy Bill?' Flora repeated. 'Is that his name?'

'That *was* his name. He's dead now . . . '

'You said a moment ago that you are Loupe Vanquera,' Flora interrupted. 'The bank robber! The bandit! The hold-up man . . . '

'Just so,' Vanquera agreed, smiling. 'Why should I not admit it to one so lovely? And, surely, you must appreciate that I cannot let you go? Think how disastrous it would be for me if you revealed where I have my headquarters — as of course you would.'

Flora stood looking at him, then beyond him to the distant slope which led away from the main street. She was wondering why nobody had followed her.

'The saloon is where I have my base,' Vanquera explained. 'The only other inhabitants of this ghost town were Crazy Bill and the youth. Now Bill is dead, and as for the boy . . . well, maybe he will take to the wilds. About all he is fit for. As for you, *señorita*, I fancy you can be useful to me. Are you not the daughter of Lanning Mackenzie, the retired banker?'

'Supposing I am?' Flora snapped.

Vanquera smiled. 'I should imagine your father would be willing to pay for your safety. Now move, please — down the street to that saloon.'

Flora hesitated for a moment, until she realized she just had to obey. She started walking, pausing again as she saw the dead body of Crazy Bill lying before her. Vanquera turned and signalled his henchman.

'Get rid of that,' he ordered.

The gunman in the rear nodded — and Flora went on walking through the thick dust and rapidly deepening shadows. She gained the boardwalk outside the saloon and passed through the batwings into the gloomy interior. Then at a word from Vanquera she stopped, his gun pressing lightly into her spine. Presently he removed it and she turned to face him.

'I have no need to continue my vigilance, *señorita*,' he explained. 'You will make no attempt to leave this saloon; there are too many of us to watch you.'

After a glance about her Flora realized what he meant. The old, half-wrecked saloon with its ancient — and in places crumbled — furniture contained perhaps half a dozen gunmen. They were in various parts of the big, cobwebby expanse, crouched in the fast deepening shadows of the approaching night. They reminded Flora of rats which had run to cover.

'These men are my friends,' Vanquera explained, then with a hardening of his mouth he added: 'Or at least I know them. I don't doubt but what any of them would kill me at the first opportunity if I once relaxed . . . '

He pulled forth a chair, dusted it with his hat, then motioned Flora to be seated. She obeyed because there was nothing else she could do, but all the time her eyes kept darting about for a possible way of escape.

'Drink for the lady,' the bandit

ordered, glancing towards his men. 'And hurry it up! What is your choice, Miss Mackenzie?'

'I have none.'

'Why be foolish?' Vanquera smiled. 'In this climate one has a perpetual thirst. It shall be wine, and I shall join you. When we took over this ruin we found its cellars still well stocked. As for food . . . ' He shrugged. 'The last time we were in Mowry City we took care to remove all we would need for a long time to come. Being outlaws,' he finished drily, 'one has to look ahead.'

Flora did not say anything. When the wine had been brought by one of the gunmen she took the filled glass Vanquera handed to her.

'I suppose,' she said, as she sipped the wine slowly, 'it was you who I saw up on the mountainside as we moved in to settle our base camp?'

'So I am getting careless?' Vanquera asked in surprise. 'I actually revealed myself?'

'I caught a glimpse of you for a

moment — and let me tell you something, Vanquera. Keeping me here you're asking for trouble. Before very long my friends in the camp will come looking for me.'

Vanquera chuckled. 'Yes, I expect they will — but they will not reach here. I have other men than these, *señorita*. In fact I have to have, so that instant warning can be given in case of danger. I have left them with orders to prevent any attempt at rescuing you.'

'You mean you'd shoot my friends?' Flora gasped.

'Possibly.' Vanquera gave his hard smile. 'I have my own interests to protect, Miss Mackenzie, and I certainly do not care whether or not your friends live or die. In fact, when I consider that aunt of yours I think I might do humanity a service by removing her. And she is your aunt, I believe? You see, I know so much about you.'

Flora put down her glass, half emptied, on the dusty top of the nearby table. She gave the outlaw a direct look.

'*How* do you know so much about me?'

'I make a point of knowing all the important people in the region in which I happen to be. I know the names and habits of all the ranchers around here, which includes your father. As I said earlier, I think he will pay well for the safe return of his daughter.'

'I take it you were not afraid of Crazy Bill knowing you and your men were here?'

'No.' Vanquera studied his wine for a moment. 'Crazy Bill never left the town: he was too imbecilic. He lived in one of the shacks at the limit of the town, that boy working for him. The boy was treated pretty much as a slave, as far as I could discover . . . However, that does not concern us. Since the town is now empty save for myself and my boys — not forgetting you, *señorita* — I am well satisfied.'

Flora got to her feet in sudden

determination. 'You can't keep me here, Vanquera! You can only stop me by shooting me, and if you think I'm so valuable you won't do that. I'm going right now . . . '

'I think not.' Vanquera's hand closed tightly round her arm. 'And I would suggest, *señorita*, that you think more clearly. If you *go*, I shall lose you anyway, so I'll have no compunction about shooting you. Since you will not be tractable I have only one course . . . '

And without further argument he swung the protesting girl round, bundled her fiercely across the dusty saloon, and finally pitched her into an adjoining room which had obviously once been an office. She collided with an ancient chair and then collapsed on the floor.

'I dislike treating a lady roughly,' Vanquera said, looking down on her. 'You force me to it, *señorita*. You can have every consideration if you will co-operate.'

'Co-operate in what?' Flora half lay

71

on the floor, tossing the hair back from her face.

'Is it so difficult to understand?' the outlaw asked. 'Until your father pays for your safe return we must, of necessity, be together for some time. I see no reason why we cannot know each other . . . better.'

The frozen look of disgust he received made him raise his eyebrows. He shrugged and turned back towards the door.

'Hunger and thirst may bring you to my way of thinking,' he commented, as he went out. Then the ancient key turned in the lock and Flora was left in the growing darkness.

4

Flora's continued absence only became noticeable to Dick, Black Moon and Aunt Belinda after perhaps an hour. Until this time pride had kept Dick from following her, and the redskin and Belinda were too busy to notice anything, anyway. But as the shadows lengthened and there was no sign of the girl returning, Dick began to look about him from sorting out the implements for the next day's work.

'Where do you suppose Flora is all this time?' he called across to Belinda, and her enormous stooped rear gave place to her face.

'Mopin', like as not,' she answered. 'Gals like her is all alike. Say somethin' they don't mean and then they feel ready t'cut their tongues out.'

'Twilight's coming,' Dick said, glancing upwards at the mountain faces. 'I don't like the idea of Flora being left to fend for herself when it gets dark. I guess I'd better see where she is.'

Belinda considered for a moment, then cupping her mouth with horny hands she bawled 'Flora!' with such power that the mountains echoed it again and again. She tried twice more, but there came no response. Dick's lips tightened.

'That does it!' he said. 'She's out of earshot — and that means a pretty good distance with the noise you can make, Belinda. Moony, you'd better come with me. Tracking is in your line.'

The Indian nodded and came over to Dick's side. Together they began to move towards the spot where they had last seen the girl. Before they had covered a dozen yards Belinda had caught up with them, her umbrella gripped firmly in her right hand.

'Yuh don't reckon yuh can leave me alone, do yuh?' she demanded.

'Why not?' Dick muttered. 'Somebody ought to stay and take care of the horses and the camp. I remember Flora saying she thought she saw somebody on the rimrock as we came into the pass.'

'All the more reason why I should stick with you two,' Belinda snorted. 'I ain't afraid of a fair fight, but when it comes to watchin' a whole camp I'd be loco to do it alone. I'm only a woman, when yuh've finished.'

Black Moon and Dick exchanged looks of wonder but passed no comment. Then they came to the top of the rise, and the rock spur beyond which Flora had last been seen to vanish. There was no sign of her anywhere in the expanse.

'Where the devil can she have gone?' Dick demanded, in growing alarm. 'Moony, what about footprints?'

The redskin was already looking at the dust. 'No trail,' he announced. 'Wind keep dust on move. Prints go fast as made.'

He contemplated the landscape for a while.

'Well?' Dick asked anxiously. 'Any hope?'

'Footprints not help Black Moon,' the Indian said. 'The white squaw could not have gone north: we see her from camp. And not up mountain face. So white squaw went ahead. I . . . '

Black Moon stopped abruptly, his dark eyes fixed on something on the cliff face above him. He stood as rigid as a statue for a moment, then he abruptly dived forward to the shelter of the rocks, dragging Dick and Belinda with him, as there was a sudden rifle shot. His prompt action definitely saved either Dick or Belinda from injury, for dust spat viciously where they had been standing.

'Evidently Flora wasn't dreaming when she said she saw somebody,' Dick snapped, whipping out his gun. 'I'm going to get that critter, whoever it is. It's also pretty certain he saw where Flora went. Probably we can make him talk.'

'Unless he's shot the gal an' dragged

her body outa sight somewheres,' Belinda commented, genuinely worried for once.

'We are being watched,' Black Moon grunted. 'Black Moon not surprised — with gold near. Camp show what we intend doing. Black Moon deal with watcher,' he added, drawing out his wickedly sharp hunting knife and then putting it between his teeth. 'Wait . . . '

Dick nodded slowly, knowing full well that he would stand little chance in trying to scale the mountain face, even though the dimness of the light might have helped him somewhat. So he relaxed in the cover of the rocks, Belinda beside him, and they both watched the Indian glide over the ledge of rock close by, and then he began to worm his way upwards.

The manner in which he climbed was entirely individual. He found toe and finger holds in the smallest spaces and ascended so quietly he might have been a shadow, his close-fitting clothes not disturbing the smallest stone. All the time he kept his eyes fixed above, but since there was no sign of attack he judged correctly that his flatness against the rocks prevented him being observed.

So at length he gained the narrow ledge from where the shot had come. Keeping in the cover of a huge boulder he eased himself around it and peered along the yard-wide mountain trail. There were two men there in the dying light, both of them with rifles, their attention fixed on the expanse below, evidently waiting for Dick, Belinda and Black Moon to appear.

The Indian took the knife from his teeth. He held finger and thumb lightly over the vicious point and gently waved the knife back and forth — then it flew from his fingers with savage force. The nearer man received it clean in the neck. It tore into his jugular and buried itself to the hilt. Choked with blood, his breath strangling in his throat, he reeled backwards into the dust.

Black Moon hurtled forward at the

same instant as the knife landed. The second gunman whirled round and tried to take aim with his rifle, but it was too clumsy a weapon for such quick action. The Indian was upon him before he could steady himself. A blinding uppercut whirled the gunman backwards, his jaw feeling as though it had been smashed from its hinge.

He made an effort to recover himself but instead his arms were seized and forced relentlessly up his back. He was crushed down on to his knees, a tremendous pressure weighing down upon his spine.

'Black Moon kill unless white man speak,' the Indian warned. 'Paleface tell Black Moon where white squaw is hidden.'

'I'm not tellin' no dirty Indian nothin'!' the gunhawk panted, pain making him gasp. 'I don't know what — Hell!' he broke off in anguish, as his arms were forced further back.

'Black Moon break arm, and then back, if paleface not speak,' the redskin murmured. 'Where is white squaw?'

For a second or two the gunhawk did not answer, then the slowly increasing pressure began to force words out of him.

'She's — she's with the boss!'

'Who is boss?' Black Moon demanded.

'Vanquera. He's in the ghost town — three miles away mebbe.'

Black Moon relaxed a little. 'Vanquera? Paleface outlaw.'

He released his hold abruptly and the gunman got up stiffly, massaging his throbbing arms. Then he stared blankly as he realized that Black Moon had recovered his knife from the body of the man lying a few feet away. The blade gleamed in the dying light.

'White men enemies of Black Moon,' the Indian said deliberately, his high-cheekboned face expressionless. 'Black Moon not like you. Black Moon kill you.'

'But you can't!' the man shouted hoarsely. 'I gave yuh th' infurmation yuh wanted — '

'Paleface a killer. Paleface an outlaw. Black Moon has spoken.'

The knife seemed to fly out of the Indian's fingers and embedded itself in the outlaw's breast. He took one deep breath, gazed stupidly in front of him, and then dropped. Black Moon shrugged, recovered his knife, and then turned as he heard footsteps. Dick and Belinda had followed him up the rocks.

'What's this? Wholesale slaughter?' Dick demanded blankly.

'Two whites unfit to live,' Black Moon responded. 'And we must move fast. Vanquera has white squaw. Ghost town — three miles. Black Moon never heard of ghost town.'

'Ghost town? Round here?' Belinda asked. Then she thought for a minute. Finally she snapped her fingers. 'Yeah, sure there is! I reckon it's called Hudson's Folly.'

'Hudson?' Dick repeated.

'Sure thing. A guy named Hudson built the place some years back, figgerin' he'd cash in on a gold rush. A slug in the belly changed his mind, I reckon. Reckon we'd best be on our way.'

She turned about and began the descent of the rocks, Dick and the Indian slithering down behind her. In the gloom, when she had reached the bottom of the ascent, Belinda began to stride purposefully through the dust, Dick and the Indian beside her.

'Know exactly where this place is, Belinda?' Dick asked, as they moved along.

'Not dead on the spit, but I reckon it can only be in this direction. Mountains stop it being either side.'

So, since she had become the leader, Dick and the redskin could only follow her. They seemed to keep going for an interminable time, winding in and out of the rocks, covering the same wilderness which Flora herself had traversed, until at last they came to the top of a slope which overlooked the town. By this time the night had come, as suddenly as the snuffing out of a candle.

'Look like those two guards were the only ones,' Belinda commented. 'Probably sent ter stop us leavin' camp. Don't seem to be any more uv the critters lyin' around.'

'We have to be careful all the same even with the darkness covering us,' Dick said. 'From all accounts Vanquera is a tough customer to deal with.'

He eased his gun into his hand and Black Moon fixed his deadly knife between his teeth; so Belinda took a firmer grip on her massive umbrella. Then they began moving down the long slope which led to the main street. They crouched as they advanced, hoping thereby to disguise their movements. Dark though it was, the starlight made them appear black against the all-surrounding whiteness of the dust.

'Wish we knew exactly where to look,' Dick muttered at length. 'There are quite a few buildings around here — '

'Get your hands up, the lot of you,' a voice commanded.

They all rose quickly and turned. Not very far from them, advancing from the cover of the stray rocks which lined the slope, were three men. The starlight gleamed on the barrels of their guns as they advanced.

'Well, if this ain't nice,' the foremost man commented, still coming forward. 'The rest uv the party in one little group — Okay, Shorty, hop to the boss and tell him what we've got.'

The stumpy, thick-set man to the rear of the speaker began moving swiftly through the gloom. Dick's eyes followed him, watching where he went — but he was not given the chance to see where the journey finished.

'Drop yuh gun, you!' the owl-hooter snapped at him. 'An' you open yuh teeth and let that knife fall!'

Dick obeyed, and after a moment Black Moon complied also. Belinda tightened her hold on her umbrella.

'I reckon you three must be suckers

fur trouble,' the gunman commented, and his companion gave a dry murmur of agreement. 'Yuh didn't think yuh could walk inter a town like this an' have a red carpet out fur yuh, did yuh? Only one thing puzzles me: how in heck did yuh get past the boys posted on th' rimrock near yuh camp?'

'Black Moon destroy them,' the Indian answered dispassionately. 'Black Moon kill you — soon.'

'You hope,' the gunman replied. 'Take more'n a dirty redskin t'do that — '

'Yuh cheap, low-down ornery scum!' Belinda yelled suddenly, in such noisy fury that both gunmen started. 'Who in heck d'yuh think yuh are, stealin' a gal who's done yuh no harm, an' now figgerin' on givin' us th' run around? I'll show yuh — !'

She lunged forward at the close of her sentence, her umbrella battering with violent strokes across the nearer gunman. He was so utterly unprepared for the attack that he staggered backwards, firing his gun blindly into the air. Belinda slammed at him again, back and forth across his head; then she abruptly switched to the second man and smashed the gun out of his hand before he could fire it.

Black Moon leapt, his knife back in his teeth from the dust where he had dropped it. In split seconds he had seized the man who had done most of the talking, sinking his lean, steel-strong fingers into his throat. The remaining man did his best to lend assistance until a bullet from Dick's gun dropped him in his tracks.

But it was an advantage which could not last. From not far away there came a sudden hail of shots and the explosion of guns. A voice shouted amidst the confusion:

'Take it easy there! You're all covered!'

Black Moon gave a final strangling squeeze to the throat of the gunman he was holding, then he stood up and slipped his knife back in its sheath. Dick reholstered his gun and stood with his hands raised as Shorty and four other gunmen came nearer.

'Just in time,' panted the gunman lying in the dust. 'I guess this jigger got Charley, though.'

'I'd have got you too if I'd had the chance,' Dick snapped.

Shorty motioned his gun in the starlight. 'There ain't no more time for games. The boss wants t'see yuh. Git on the move.'

There was nothing else for it. Dick, Black Moon, and Belinda finished their journey in the main saloon room. Dim oil lamps were burning, their light masked from outside by the shuttered windows. Loupe Vanquera was half seated on one of the ancient tables. Behind him, a couple of men lazed in the shadows, ready for instant action if need be.

'Good evening, friends,' the outlaw greeted, as the trio came into the area of the lamp.

'Mind if I spit in yuh eye?' Belinda asked sourly.

'If you are prepared to receive a bullet in return, no,' Vanquera answered calmly. 'I must congratulate you on having got this far. I never thought you would. Perhaps, though, it might help to raise the price. I imagine Mr Mackenzie will be willing to pay more for four than for one.'

'Ransom, huh?' Belinda asked bitterly. 'So that's what yuh game is?'

'Partly . . . I have also other reasons for holding you and Miss Mackenzie. I want to know just what you are doing in the pass yonder.'

None of the three spoke. Vanquera considered them and then gave his broad smile.

'I realize that all three of you are tough enough to keep quiet no matter how persuasive I might become. But I wonder if the same could be said of Miss Mackenzie?'

'What the hell are you driving at?' Dick demanded. 'What have you done to that girl?'

'As yet — nothing. She's in the next

room, and she will stay there for as long as I see fit. You three will also join her. But I am curious to know what you are in this district for. I noticed you had digging equipment and camp requirements, for quite a long stay. I suppose you wouldn't be intending to look for — gold?'

Still the three remained silent. Vanquera's mouth hardened and he stood upright. Abruptly the flat of his hand struck Dick across the face so violently that he staggered.

'I like my questions answered,' the outlaw said harshly. 'Are you looking for gold?'

'Who isn't?' Dick rubbed his tingling cheek.

Vanquera hesitated for a moment; then he lighted a long Mexican cheroot and drew on it thoughtfully.

'My guess is that you're searching for the gold lost in the stagecoach disaster of fifteen years ago,' he said. 'A consignment worth two hundred thousand dollars was buried under a landfall

— a consignment from the Mackenzie Bank. I know all about that, as most folk do around this region. The fact that Flora Mackenzie is with you makes me certain that you are looking for gold. I would have done it myself long ago only I don't know exactly where to look. That being so, I could waste a great deal of time and energy and expose myself to lawmen who are still hunting for me. With you, and Miss Mackenzie, it is different. You know where to look.'

Dick shook his head. 'We don't. There's no point in trying to hide the fact that we are looking for that lost gold, but we've no more idea than you where it is.'

'I don't believe you!' Vanquera retorted. 'Let me tell you what I am going to do . . . You will work for me from here on. You will find that gold, and you will be kept under cover of guns from all sides as you work. Since you have come on an expedition for the sole purpose of hunting gold nobody will come and look for you; and if by some chance they should, that will be taken care of. I shall leave the matter of ransom until later. It would defeat my own ends if the ransom were paid and I had to send you back . . . '

The outlaw took his cheroot from his teeth and studied it.

'But I give you warning,' he added slowly, looking at the three each in turn. 'If you do not come to the gold after one day of digging, which you most certainly should since you know exactly where to look, I will take steps to put an end to your stalling. And I think Miss Mackenzie will have the least resistance. You understand?'

'If yuh think yuh'll git anythin' out uv us, yore crazy!' Belinda declared, and thumped the ferrule of her umbrella on the floor. 'We can't just guarantee ter hit gold in a given time. Mebbe weeks, mebbe — '

'One day! That's all!' the outlaw interrupted. 'Otherwise you'll be in for an unpleasant time. I want that gold first and the ransom afterwards. Since I have to lie low in this region for the time being I may as well turn it to account. Tomorrow you start digging . . . Tonight you shall have food, drink, and rest. Shorty, get the horses from that base camp and bring them in.'

★ ★ ★

After they had been given their meal — beans and coffee at which Flora was permitted to join them, the four found themselves bundled into the adjoining office, the door being locked upon them. In the dark, seated on the floor, they were left to their own devices.

'What's the answer to this one, Moony?' Dick asked after a while.

'Black Moon no answer,' the Indian growled.

'That's a good one, coming from you. Usually you can think your way out of a tight corner. Do you think we can escape from in here? The wall's only wood, and probably not very strong. Or we might move the boarding from over that window there.'

Dick glanced to where starlight was showing through chinks in the planks.

'We've no weapons,' Black Moon said. 'My knife and your gun — outlaw take. Outside, many gunmen on watch.'

'Then we just do as we're told?' Flora demanded. 'Tomorrow we start digging for gold, and if we don't find it we're supposed to say where it is. How can we when we don't know? Vanquera might kill the lot of us trying to get the answer, not believing we really *don't* know.'

'We'll tackle that when it comes.' Dick's voice was grim. 'For the moment it looks as though our Mexican hoodlum has the whip hand. Right now I think we can't do better than try and get some sleep. Tomorrow promises to be pretty trying.'

This, as it proved, was an understatement. At sunup the four found themselves awakened. They were given breakfast of sorts, then they marched out into the brilliant sunlight and were

93

told to get on their horses — which Shorty had brought over for the night. In half an hour they were back at their base camp, followed by Vanquera and five of his men.

'You know where that gold is and you can dig straight to it,' the outlaw said, when the torrid expanse of the one-time pass had been reached. 'Get it! We will be watching from different points, so don't try anything. I am seeing to it that we are not visible to anybody who might try and approach.'

With that, he and his men took up various positions amongst the rocks, leaving the quartet to collect their picks and shovels. They looked at one another hopelessly and then began to move . . .

★   ★   ★

And at almost the same moment Lanning Mackenzie was giving final instructions to his ranch foreman.

'Don't know how long I'll be away, Bart,' he said, 'but I know I can rely on you in the interval.'

'You sure can, Mr Mackenzie,' agreed the lean, leathery being who ruled the Lazy-G outfit.

'No use my saying I can keep my nose out of this business,' Mackenzie smiled. 'I just can't . . . I keep thinking of Flora up there in the mountains, probably having a grand holiday while the gold search is on, and I'm playing about down here doing nothing in particular. I might as well join them.'

The foreman nodded and Mackenzie turned to his ready-loaded horse. He swung easily into the saddle, settled his big Stetson on his head, and then rode out of the yard . . .

He stopped at noon to rest the horse and have a meal; then again he went on: It was not far from six o'clock when his long, hard ride began to come to an end and he had the slope leading to the one-time pass straight in front of him. He was feeling pleased with himself and all the world. Even if he had got past the age when he could have taken his share in the digging, he could at least watch and attend to other details — such as the care of the camp. In any case, he had found it quite intolerable to stay behind at the ranch and wait for something to happen.

He came presently to the top of the slope and looked about him. Not observing anything living he kept on going, and at last was rewarded by a distant vision of four figures, digging steadily in the white dust. He halted his mount, leaned on the saddle-horn, and gazed at the quartet. Hidden amongst the rocks, Vanquera and his men did not observe him — but Dick did suddenly, and gave a start.

'There's your dad,' he murmured to Flora, and she looked up in surprise. She was so weary with a day of back-breaking effort in blinding sunlight that she could hardly concentrate.

'Dad?' she repeated; and then she saw the horseman. 'Dick, if he calls to us he's done for! Vanquera and his men can't see him at the moment, but if they do — '

'Don't signal,' Belinda interrupted, working and watching Mackenzie in the distance. 'Give him the tip-off with your shovel, son. Use Morse. I know he understands it, being a banker.'

Actually, Mackenzie was puzzled. Certainly he did not grasp that the words — D-A-N-G-E-R — K-E-E-P C-L-E-A-R were being transmitted to him as Dick hacked away at the edge of a big stone, sending out the clanging series of signals.

Mackenzie was right on the verge of shouting; then he paused at the sight of three gunmen moving from the rock cover to where the quartet was working.

'What's the idea?' Vanquera asked Dick bluntly.

'Of what?' Dick stopped hitting the stone and looked up, deliberately engaging the outlaw's atention so he would not glance behind him towards the lone horseman in the distance.

'Hitting that stone with your shovel.

You're wasting time, and I don't like it! The day's nearly done, and how far have you got? Nowhere!'

Dick hesitated, his eyes on Vanquera's gun. By looking at it he could see out of the tail of his eye if the horseman was still there. He was not. Mackenzie had vanished.

'All right, keep on digging,' the outlaw snapped, moving back to the rock shelter again. 'You've only your-selves to thank for what will happen if you don't find that gold in the time limit I set.'

'Time limit be dad-blamed!' Belinda declared fiercely, spitting into the dust. 'We've sweated around here all day lookin' fur th' blasted gold, an' found nothin'. Why can't yuh git it inter yuh addled skull that if there's gold around here it may take weeks ter find it?'

'You know just where it is!' Vanquera retorted. 'An' what I said before still goes. If yuh don't find it I'll make Miss Mackenzie talk!'

With that Vanquera completed his

retreat and sat down amongst the rocks with his gun cocked. He glanced at his colleagues and grinned.

'They'll find it,' he said confidently. 'Just stallin' an' if they don't it's surprising what you can do with a girl as a lever.'

'Just s'pose they *don't* find it?' Shorty asked, his eyes narrowed on the quartet. 'That gal might prove tougher'n we expect.'

'Not with my methods,' Vanquera answered, lighting a Mexican cheroot one-handedly.

Meantime the four were working in a tight little bunch, perspiring freely, shovelling with all their strength.

'If we *could* find some gold it would save an awful lot of trouble,' Dick commented. 'Otherwise I don't dare to think what might happen to you, Flora.'

'Let them ornery jiggers put a hand on her an' I'll kill 'em!' Belinda vowed.

'That's just talk,' Dick said irritably. 'They've gotten the whip hand of us, and our only chance is to find gold. Better dig as hard and fast as we can.'

'Black Moon wonder where white man go,' Black Moon remarked, stripped to the waist, his lithe body gleaming in the sunlight.

'Evidently he got the hang of my message,' Dick answered. 'Our only hope is to drag things out and maybe he'll bring help.'

Which was just what Lanning Mackenzie was aiming to do. Though he had not understood the message he had seen that the quartet was in the hands of desperadoes; so he rode hard under the evening sun, heading for Buzzard's Bend, ten miles east of Springerville, and the nearest point where a sheriff could be contacted.

But Mackenzie was no longer a young man and he had already had a tough day of riding. Several times on the way he had to stop and rest, which made it after sundown before he gained the ramshackle town of Buzzard's

Bend. He rode straight to the sheriff's office in the kerosene-lighted main street and found the place shut. In the town's only saloon, however, he had better luck. The sheriff was standing at the bar counter, a glass of rye at his elbow.

He — and the many customers — gave Mackenzie a curious glance as he walked unsteadily from the batwings and ordered a double brandy from the barkeep.

'Ridin' hard, stranger?' the sheriff enquired.

Mackenzie swallowed some of the brandy, and felt better. The sheriff was a big man, hard-mouthed, with curiously oblique grey eyes which gave him the look of constant surprise.

'Riding hard, yes,' Mackenzie agreed. 'To find you. Get your deputies and a posse together: we're riding on back to Skeleton Pass in the Mongos. Vanquera's hiding there — and he's got my daughter, sister-in-law, and a couple of friends as captives.'

The sheriff looked at his rye, then back to Mackenzie's tired but earnest features.

'Y'mean Vanquera the outlaw? The Mexican?'

'That's right. I saw him myself, and I'd know him anywheres after seeing his picture on the reward-dodgers up and down the state. Better get saddled and ride back with me.'

'Yeah . . . Yeah, sure thing.' The sheriff swallowed his rye and wiped the back of his hand over his mouth. 'I'll meet you outside,' he promised, and hurried away.

Mackenzie finished the remainder of his brandy, decided he felt less shaky, and made for the batwings again. Outside, he released his horse's reins from the tie-rack and then led the animal down the street to the trough. He had also given it some fodder by the time the sheriff and his men came riding up. There were six of them, every one apparently hard-baked, cross-overs swinging from their hips as they sat straight in their saddles.

'Might help a bit, old-timer, if I knew yuh name,' the sheriff said. 'Mine's Friar.'

'Lanning Mackenzie,' Mackenzie said, climbing to his saddle.

'Seem to have heard of yuh,' the sheriff mused. 'A banker, ain't yuh?'

'I was until I retired. Now come on, will you? I'm worrying as to what may be happening.'

He nudged his horse forward, leading the way, but the animal was far too tired to do anything but a jog trot. In a group to the rear the sheriff and his men followed on, the men glancing at each other and smiling significantly, then looking at Mackenzie's back ahead of them.

The barrenness of the trail had been reached, the dawning moonlight just commencing to pick out the vast pasture lands and distant mountains, when Mackenzie realized that the sheriff and his men had not only caught up with him but were surrounding him.

'Stop a minnit, Mackenzie,' Friar ordered.

Mackenzie obeyed, frowning. 'What's the idea?' he demanded. 'I keep telling you that — '

'Yeah, sure thing. That yuh daughter, sister-in-law, and a coupla mugs are captives of Vanquera. S'pose we get your daughter back for yuh safely — how much is it worth to yuh?'

'What the devil are you talking about, man? You're a sheriff! You've got your duty to do!'

'Sure. But I have my own ways of working.'

Mackenzie breathed hard. 'Trying to pull something, eh?' he demanded.

'You're a banker, Mackenzie — and a rich man. Most people in the state know that. Yuh can afford some of that money of yourn to get your kid back. I don't guarantee to rescue the other mugs, whoever they are, but I will try and get your daughter back to yuh safely. That is, if it's worth fifty thousand dollars to yuh.'

It took Mackenzie a little while to realize that he had fallen into the hands of a decidedly crooked sheriff — and, alone, there was not much he could do about it, except speak his mind.

'You know what will happen to you, Friar, if this gets to the ears of the Federal authorities?'

'Yuh feel like telling 'em, mebbe?' the sheriff asked drily.

'I'll darned well see that you're blasted out of office!'

'Yeah? That how much yuh value yuh kid?'

Mackenzie was silent, his face grim in the starlight.

'Better git wise to yuhself, Mackenzie,' Friar said. 'I'll try and get yuh kid fur yuh, like I sed — but only fur fifty thousand dollars. Where do yuh hang out? — I fergit.'

'The Lazy-G, five miles north of Mowry City, New Mexico,' Mackenzie muttered.

'Good enough fur me. Tell yuh what yuh do. You have that money in thousand-dollar bills made up in a parcel an' tie it to the main gate uv yuh ranch. When it's bin found and taken away yuh daughter will be sent back to you, unharmed. But I'll also have men covering her so that if you try and get my boys while the money's being taken she'll get a bullet straight through her heart. Understand?'

'You don't expect me to lie low and keep quiet after she has been returned, do you?' Mackenzie snapped. 'I'll go for you with all I've got, Friar! Once I've paid for her safe return our bargain's over. I'll have you arrested for extortion and blackmail!'

'Yeah?' Friar chuckled heavily. 'Just try doin' it, Mackenzie, and bring all the proof yuh can. Won't be so easy, I reckon, with no witnesses around to what we're sayin' now. I'm going to blame all this on Vanquera, an' don't yuh forget it!'

Mackenzie, fighter though he was, knew when he was beaten. Gambling with the life of Flora was something he could not do. He spoke quietly.

'Very well, Friar, you win. The money will be put on the gate when I get back home. I'm starting right now. And if you don't get my daughter in return for the money I'll have every marshal in the country on the prod for you.'

'I'll keep my end up,' Friar retorted. 'Now blow! Yuh'll get yuh kid soon enough.'

Mackenzie said no more. He turned his horse's head and the weary animal began to lope forward along the trail until it was lost to sight.

5

'What's the idea?' one of Friar's men demanded presently. 'What makes yuh so sure yuh can do a deal with Vanquera? He's about the toughtest guy loose in the state!'

'A man who's as much wanted as he is can't afford ter be choosy,' Friar answered briefly. 'Any time I want I can put th' finger on him, an' he knows it. He's only hanging out in the Mongols at all 'cos I let him. Yuh don't suppose I don't know his men come inter Buzzard's Bend fur provisions, do yuh? That guy'll do as I tell him — an' like it.'

'An' how's about the fifty thousand?' another of the men asked.

'We split it between us. Half fur me, and you mugs can split the remainder between yuh.'

'Yeah? Now wait a minnit — '

'Shut up!' Friar spat. 'I'm runnin' this outfit an' don't go fergettin' it. Any time I can clamp any of you guys in the hoosegow fur things yuh've done — or had yuh forgotten?'

His men were silent. Each one of them was wanted for some crime or other, but they still had liberty because Friar allowed it. It suited his purpose to have under his thumb men whom he could blackmail into serving him.

'Okay, we'll be on our way,' he said at length. 'We can cut across country. Let's go —'

He whirled his horse's head round, stabbed in the spurs viciously, darting the animal from the trail to the grass bank. Thereafter he set a furious pace through the night, thundering over pasture lands with his men not far behind him. The animals were well rested and capable of the strain of a long ride. It was as well they were for Friar never once permitted a halt until the Mongolian Range was reached; then he began to ride more slowly, one of his guns drawn in case a look-out happened to think he was an enemy and fired before he could explain.

'How th' heck d'yuh reckon t'find Vanquera in this set-up?' one of the men grumbled. 'We might search these blasted mountains fur weeks and get no place.'

'Use yuh brains,' Friar growled. 'Yuh heard Mackenzie say Vanquera was in Skeleton Pass, didn't yuh?'

'Nope. I wusn't there.'

The sheriff spat. 'Anyways, that's where he is. An' that's a goodish way through these foothills.'

He urged his horse forward at a faster pace, following the rough, rubbly ground at the base of the mountains, moving all the time in the direction of Skeleton Pass. The hard going, however, made it at least another hour before the depression which had been a pass was reached. Here Friar drew rein and looked about him in the moonlight.

'Full uv dust an' nothin' else,' one of the men grunted. 'I can't see Vanquera bein' loco enough to stick around here. Mebbe Mackenzie handed yuh a bum steer, sheriff?'

'I reckon not. He'd no reason to. We'd better take a look around.'

Friar started his horse on the move again, the animal's hoofs churning the white dust of the once famous pass. For nearly an hour and a half Friar and his grumbling men explored the region before they picked up footprints — several of them — in the soft ground. After that, tracking them back in the bright moonlight, it was not long before they came in sight of the ghost town.

'Now I get it,' Friar murmured, leaning on the saddle horn and gazing at the distant buildings, white under the moon and stars. 'This dump's known as Hudson's Folly — bin deserted fur years. Couldn't be a better hideout fur Vanquera, I guess. He'll be there someplace.'

He started riding down the slope, but had not got far before a rifle exploded in the silence. A bullet whanged not a yard away.

'Take it easy, fellas!' a voice shouted from concealment. 'Say what yore doin' around here, an' say it quick!'

Friar halted, signalling his men to do likewise. He cupped his hands.

'Where do I find Vanquera? I've important news fur him. I'm Sheriff Friar of Buzzard's Bend.'

'A *sheriff?* Yuh'd better keep goin', fella. Yuh'll find him in the saloon. That's his headquarters. Step outa line and yuh'll be drilled and no questions asked. There's men fixed all the way.'

Muttering to himself Friar kept on riding, to presently gain the ghost town's main street. His hammering on the door of the saloon brought a man with levelled gun to open it. Beyond him was the oil-lighted expanse of the saloon itself.

'Sheriff Friar — and men,' Friar said briefly. 'I've got ter see Vanquera on business.'

'Better be good business,' the gunman

answered coldly. 'Okay, come right in. There's the boss.'

He motioned his weapon and Friar looked about him in the yellow glow. The windows were tightly shuttered. In the big area of the one-time saloon men were lounging, some of them playing cards, others half asleep. In a chair by himself, cleaning his gun, was Vanquera. He looked up, a cynical grin on his swarthy face.

'Come right in, sheriff. And you won't go out again, either, without being very convincing.'

Friar paused before the outlaw and eyed him grimly.

'I'm here to make a deal, Vanquera,' he snapped.

'A deal? The only deals I make are on my terms, sheriff.'

'Don't be too sure of that. I'm a sheriff, in the nearest town to here. If I wanted I could run you in!'

Vanquera laughed and examined his gun carefully. Since he added no words, the contempt with which he was being treated made Friar colour angrily.

'Don't think I couldn't!' he shouted. 'I've got authority!'

'In this town, my friend, you haven't got anything except the clothes you stand up in . . . and you won't even have those if I don't like your conversation . . . Now get to the point!'

Friar tightened his lips and glanced about him upon the hard-faced outlaws.

'If yore interested, I can do a deal with Lanning Mackenzie fur the safe return of his daughter.'

Vanquera squinted down the barrel of his gun critically.

'I said . . . '

'I heard you,' the outlaw interrupted. 'I'd like to know what gave you the notion you can make deals over my property.'

'*Your* property!' Friar exploded. 'Mackenzie's daughter isn't your property. She's . . . '

'At the moment she is under my protection,' Vanquera said, standing up and holstering his gun. 'How much else did you tell Mackenzie?'

'I didn't tell him anything: he told me. He asked me to ride out here and get you. I let him think I was going to, then I figgered it would be better to get money out of him, return his daughter, and leave you untouched.'

Vanquera grinned again, his white teeth shining.

'And am I supposed to believe that?'

'It's true, Vanquera!' Friar was commencing to lose his self-assurance.

'Why the desire to protect me? You're a sheriff. You could get a big reward for running me in — yet you don't. Can't be for love, so what's back of it?'

'Money,' Friar replied. 'The reward for running you in is fixed at five thousand dollars. Why should I bother with that when, by a business deal, I can make ten thousand — and you ten thousand besides.'

Vanquera lighted a cheroot. 'Make it clearer.'

'Simple enough. I fixed the ransom

figure at twenty thousand dollars. We split both ways and the girl gets returned to her old man. I reckon y'can't keep her here anyways.'

'I do as I please,' Vanquera stated. 'Where's the money to be left?'

'That's my business. I made the deal.'

'I'll give you ten seconds,' Vanquera said briefly, and drew on his cheroot, his dark eyes fixed on Friar's grim face.

'Stop clownin' around, man!' Friar complained. 'This is one helluva chance to clean, up. Ten thousand fur . . .'

'Chicken feed,' Vanquera interrupted. 'Even if the amount is right, which I doubt, there's nothing to stop you turning me in afterwards, now you know where I am, and collecting another five thousand. I wasn't born yesterday, Friar . . . Now, where's that money to be put?'

Friar began to sweat. He looked at his men helplessly, but there was nothing they could do. They believed they stood a better chance by keeping discreetly silent. Vanquera's own men, however, had moved from their various positions and formed into a circle. Friar read no pity in their steadily watching eyes.

'Where?' Vanquera asked again, blowing smoke into Friar's face.

Friar still did not answer. He was just beginning to realize that he had walked straight into a trap. Thinking only of his own personal gain he had overlooked the complete ruthlessness of the man he was dealing with.

'Get busy on him, Nick,' Vanquera said finally, and stood aside.

Friar found himself pounced upon. Though he fought and squirmed he stood no chance against three powerful gunhawks. His weapons were taken from him, he was flung into a chair, then ropes were bound with savage tightness about him. The one referred to as Nick grinned and rolled up his sleeves on steel-hard forearms.

'Nick has the strongest fingers in the States,' Vanquera explained, moving over to face the now obviously frightened sheriff. 'He'll give you a demonstration, entirely free.'

Nick grinned all the wider and stretched his hands forward. His fingers locked at the back of Friar's head, but his thumbs pressed with devastating power at the roots of the sheriff's nose. For a second or two Friar did not feel anything untoward, then as the pressure increased gradually, the anguish of tightening nerve-centres set him struggling madly, but futilely. Pain began to spread the length and breadth of his face as the inexorable thumbs continued to crush.

'He can go on for quite a long time yet,' Vanquera said, removing his cheroot from his teeth. 'You can fix the limit, Friar. I'll stand around and watch.'

Perspiration was rolling down Friar's tortured face. It was gleaming too, on Nick's unholy, smiling features as he tensed his grip harder and harder. Friar's men looked at one another and licked their lips — then at last the tearing torment brought a scream from Friar.

'Stop it! Stop it, for God's sake! I'll tell yuh!'

Vanquera nodded and Nick stood up and waited. Friar groaned, his head lolling, his hair matted with sweat. The blow across the face he received from Vanquera brought him back to life.

'Well?' the outlaw asked. 'Where will the money be?'

'The — the corral gatepost. The Lazy-G, near Mowry City.'

'And what's the real amount?'

'I — I told yuh!' Friar shouted. 'Twenty thousand dol . . . '

'Soften him up, Nick!' Vanquera ordered. 'He's a dirty liar!'

'No! No, wait!' Friar gave a gulp. 'I'll tell yuh. It wus fifty thousand . . . '

Silence. Friar began to breathe hard. Vanquera returned his cheroot to his teeth and reflected. Friar's men shifted uneasily.

'Untie him,' the outlaw ordered at length; then when the ropes had been cast free Friar found himself hauled up by the front of his shirt, Vanquera's swarthy, cynical face only a foot away from his own.

'That's — that's gospel truth, Vanquera,' Friar panted.

'I don't doubt it, you low-down chiseller. So you tried to gyp me out of thirty thousand dollars, eh? As a businessman, Friar, you're not a great success.'

'Okay, so I tried a double-cross,' the sheriff admitted. 'Yuh know the truth now. Take what yuh want an' give me a cut. I'll be satisfied.'

Vanquera looked around him at his grinning men.

'He'll be satisfied,' he remarked sourly. Then he swung back on Friar savagely. 'Why, you cheap, two-timing bushwhacker, do you think I'd do a deal with you? Do you think I'd be crazy enough to let you leave here and spill it around where me and my boys are? I guess there's only one answer, Friar.'

The sheriff's startled eyes flashed to Vanquera's gun as he whipped it from its holster.

'Waita minnit . . . ' Friar started to say, but he got no further. Vanquera fired twice and then watched the sheriff's heavy body drop. With a shrug the outlaw blew the fuming smoke from the gun barrel and re-leathered his weapon.

'Best thing, boss,' Nick said. 'Like yuh sed, the guy could have shouted his face off.'

Vanquera raised his dark eyes to look at the men who had come with Friar. They looked back at him like animals facing a snake.

'I'm a fair man,' he said finally, after drawing pensively at his cheroot. 'You probably followed Friar because he made you. It doesn't make sense to kill the lot of you when you can be useful. Take your choice: join my outfit or follow Friar to hell.'

None of the men hesitated for a moment. They relaxed and grinned uncomfortably.

'Guess we'll follow you, Vanquera,' the first deputy said.

'It also means,' the outlaw added, 'that if the law ever catches up — as it might one day — you'll go down with me. Got that?'

The men's expressions changed a little but they still nodded. Death later was better than death now.

'All right, give your names to Shorty,' Vanquera said, nodding to his shifty-eyed henchman. 'And get this body outside and buried,' he added to Nick.

There was a general movement as his orders were followed out, then he stood thinking hard. Presently Shorty turned to him, at the end of taking down the names of Friar's cohorts.

'What about those four, boss?' he asked, nodding towards the room adjoining the saloon. 'There's fifty thousand waitin' fur the pickin' up.

Seems t'me we oughta do somethin' about it.'

'You telling me what to do?' Vanquera snapped coldly.

'Nope, but it only seems common sense ter . . .'

'To get your hands on fifty thousand? I expected that! Try anything like that, Shorty, and I'll split your skull three ways . . . This wants thinking about,' the outlaw added, his voice low as he paced thoughtfully away from the group of men. 'Those four haven't located that gold yet, and until they do I want every one of them — especially the girl. She's the best lever of the lot.'

'I could go to work on her, or Nick could,' Shorty suggested. 'Then yuh could return her to her old man an' collect the money.'

'And the other three?'

'Wipe 'em out! They know too much about us — an' I'm durned sure nobody'll be anxious to pay a reward fur 'em, specially the old woman.'

After thinking further, Vanquera

appeared to make up his mind.

'I'm taking a long ride,' he said. 'I'm going to risk breaking cover to get that fifty thousand. Old man Mackenzie can easily part with it, and he don't get his daughter in return, neither. While I'm gone, Shorty, you're in charge. Try and soften the girl up — but go easy. If you kill her, I'll kill you. She's valuable. Savvy?'

'Sure, boss.' And Shorty watched Vanquera as he turned away to make preparations for departure.

*   *   *

Lanning Mackenzie had covered perhaps half the distance along the desert trail back to his ranch and was lying exhausted near a water-hole, his tired horse sleeping beside him, when he caught the sound of drumming hoofs on the stillness of the night. Here in these great spaces the sounds were distinct even though many miles away. Mackenzie stirred, propped himself on his elbow, and peered into the white expanse in the moonlight.

'Mebbe somebody unpleasant, fella,' he murmured to his horse. 'You an' I had better get off the main trail . . . '

He unfastened the reins from the cactus bush and led the sleepy animal to a hollow behind a massive dune, holding on to the reins until the rider should have passed by. The sounds of the hoofbeats came nearer and Mackenzie drew his gun, just in case. Presently curiosity got the better of him and he scrambled to the top of the dune and lay down flat, watching the trail in the bright moonlight.

Gradually the horseman came in visible range, attired all in black, his black sombrero at an angle. It did not take Mackenzie above a few seconds to place the rakish position of the hat or the general attitude of the man.

'Vanquera,' he muttered, and slid back down the dune to his horse, listening to the hoofbeats as they died away in the distance.

The matter was a puzzle to Mackenzie. Vanquera, he knew, would never come so far out of hiding without a very real cause. True, Vanquera had Flora and the rest of her party in captivity, but why was he abroad alone? What of Sheriff Friar and his men?

'Something mighty queer going on someplace,' he confided to the horse. 'I'll take a guess that Vanquera's after only one thing — money. We'd have been home by now with the money hanging on the corral gate if we hadn't been so trail weary . . . I reckon Vanquera's in for a long wait. Meantime — what about Flora?'

Mackenzie frowned to himself. That was the real worry: his daughter. Then after a while his mind eased a little as he realized that nothing could happen to Flora if she was to be used as a bargaining weapon. But if that were so, why was she not with Vanquera at this moment, to be handed over in return for the money?

Mackenzie's mouth began to set. He

could not be sure, but it smelled mighty like a double-cross.

'I reckon we've got to change our plans, fella,' he murmured. 'I was all set to go right back and put out the money as asked. Seems that it would have been taken away and I'd have gotten nothing for it. Okay, since that's the case maybe there's another way.'

He had a good idea of what he intended doing, but he did not put the plan into operation there and then. He still needed rest, and so did the horse — and it didn't matter much how long Vanquera had to wait at the other end since Flora was not with him. Once or twice Mackenzie debated whether or not he should return to Skeleton Pass and see what he could do by himself — then he decided against it. As one man alone he did not stand a chance. No, his new plan was better.

And, an hour before dawn, rested, and his horse fed and watered, he started off again, deliberately turning away from the trail which led across the desert to Mowry City district and instead making for Tucson, sixty miles to the east.

The journey, with halts, took him until the late evening, and it finished at a lone ranch some fifteen miles out of Tucson itself. Here there sprawled the Double-Square spread, owned by Jed Oakes, the cattle dealer, and — when duty demanded — a marshal of the Federal authorities.

He himself opened the ranch-house door and looked in surprise at the dusty, weary figure drooping in the porch.

'Lan Mackenzie, as I live and breathe!' he exclaimed, seizing the old banker's hand and pumping it up and down. 'Well, it sure is some time since I saw you . . . Come right in.'

'Thanks,' Mackenzie muttered, nearly too tired to see straight. He walked into the living-room and fell into the nearest chair, passing a hand over his forehead.

'Guess you're all in, Lan,' Oakes said,

pouring out brandy. 'Here — try this.'

Mackenzie gave a grateful smile and swallowed the drink. It brought more energy back to him and he sat up. Jed Oakes stood looking down on him. He was a big man, not far from forty-six, with heavy shoulders and a generous if rather ugly face. From the very earliest days he had known Mackenzie, though the banker was by far the older man.

'Well, what's it all about?' Oakes asked. 'Or shall I have a meal rustled up for you before you begin to explain?'

'I'd be glad of the meal — but make it later,' Mackenzie replied. 'This can't wait . . . It's about Flora . . . ' and he gave the details.

Oakes sat in silence when the story was finished.

'You belong to the Feds,' Mackenzie added. 'If ever there was a job for a marshal, here it is. Do the thing properly and you'll have Vanquera and all his brood falling right into your lap, as well as rescuing Flora — which, for me, is the main consideration.'

129

'Skeleton Pass,' Oakes mused, and a new expression came to his craggy features. His gaze became faraway.

'I know what you're thinking,' Mackenzie said quietly. 'It was there that your wife and son were killed in the landslide, at the same time as I lost my gold. I suppose going to that region would revive a lot of old memories — poignant ones, too.'

'That's just the trouble,' Oakes admitted; then he took a hold of the situation again. 'However, I'm a law officer when I'm needed and personal sentiment does not enter into it. I gather you haven't reported any of this to headquarters in Tucson?'

'No, I came straight to you. I figured you'd understand the situation better than they — though I suppose they have to he told.'

'Definitely.' Oakes got to his feet. 'Best thing you can do is stay here for the time being, Lan. I'll have the wife fix up a room for you.'

'Wife?' Mackenzie looked surprised.

'Necessity, I'm afraid — not romance.' Oakes smiled wistfully. 'She's over sixty and her being just my housekeeper wasn't quite the thing, so I married her. I guess there's only ever been one real wife,' he finished shrugging.

With that he left the room. When he returned he had on his hat and a gun-belt buckled about his waist.

'I've told her,' he explained. 'She's going to bring in a meal and after that you can rely on her to handle everything. Don't go back to your own spread until you hear from me. The way things look, Vanquera will be around there and almost anything can happen, unless your boys back there have nailed him by now. Anyways, I'm going over to headquarters to get my instructions.'

Mackenzie nodded gratefully and shook hands. Knowing the capabilities of Jed Oakes he felt more easy in his mind now than since the moment when he had viewed the captive four in the pass.

He had his meal and went to bed, to

be awakened again some time after midnight. Oakes's tall, rangy form was bending over him.

'Sorry old-timer,' he apologized, 'but I thought you should know what I'm going to do. I might be away for some time. I've instructions from headquarters to go after Vanquera in whatever way I see best. I'm riding out first to your ranch to see if he's around there. If he is, I'll do what I can to rope him in. If he isn't I'll pick up his trail. I'll get Flora back somehow.'

Mackenzie held out his hand and, with a smile, Oakes shook it. Then without saying anything more he left the room, went out to his horse at the front of the dark ranch-house, and was soon on his way.

With only a couple of rests *en route* he reached the region of the Lazy-G a couple of hours before dawn. Halting his horse he sat motionless in the saddle shadowed by a clump of cedar trees, and took a careful appraisal of the landscape. Trained to study detail in the uncertain light of the moon he allowed his gaze to move very gradually in a circle, hipping round in his saddle as he studied the pasture lands to his rear.

Apparently all was quiet — only Jed Oakes knew better than trust to appearances. Descending from the saddle he unfastened his bedroll and from it took a spare shirt and Stetson hat. With small branches from the trees around him he fashioned a rough scarecrow, dressed it in the shirt and hat, and then roped it to his saddle.

'Keep going, fella,' he instructed his horse. 'Full circle, like a good boy.'

His horse pawed the ground quickly, fully trained to understand. It sped away into the distance, the scarecrow gradually taking on the outlines of a stooped rider as moonlight hid the imperfections.

Mackenzie's ranch was perhaps half a mile distant, and the galloping horse covered it at top speed — and kept on going since it had learned to move for a mile before turning back on its tracks.

Oakes stood watching intently. He knew he was taking a chance with the animal's life, but usually an enemy aims at the rider, not the horse. A horse can be valuable to friend and foe alike.

When the horse had reached the Lazy-G Oakes fully expected to hear gunfire — but nothing happened. The speeding horse faded into the moonlight, then after an interval it began to reappear, racing back. Oakes stood waiting — then he tensed and watched keenly, his eyes catching sight of a dark spot moving from a distant rise of ground. The bait had worked, though not quite in the way he had expected.

Instead of drawing fire from a possible watcher — and so giving away his position — the watcher had kept his gun silent and instead was pursuing the imagined rider at top speed. Probably he did not wish to attract atention from the outfit at the Lazy-G.

'Hurry, boy, hurry!' Oakes muttered, as his horse came flying out of the moonlight.

He need not have worried. The faithful animal was a good half-mile ahead of the pursuer when he came sweating and snorting amidst the trees. Instantly Oakes slashed through the ropes holding the dummy in place, tossed it into the long grass, then swung to the saddle and continued the fast ride as hard as he could go.

He knew exactly where he was heading. A little further on there was a small depression in the ground, lying between two slightly raised hummocks. It only needed a trap to be laid and the thing would be done.

Oakes flogged his sweating beast to the limit until he gained the steeply shelving ground just beyond the depression — then he leapt from the saddle, whisking down a lariat. Whipping his rifle from the saddle he took the chance of fouling the barrel and drove it into the earth as a stake, tying the rope to it with a slip-knot. The other end he held in his hands. Lying flat, he waited for things to happen.

Nor were they long in doing so. The sound of the pursuing hoofs increased with every moment, louder, and louder still. Oakes took the gamble that for the shortest cut the purser would take the lower ground between the hummocks — and he did. Possibly he caught a glimpse of the upstanding rifle in the moonlight, but by then it was too late. Oakes pulled the rope taut.

Down went the horse, its legs tangled in the lariat, flinging the rider through the air. He landed with a thud on his back and rolled a few feet. By the time he had recovered from his daze, and his snorting horse had risen, Oakes was standing over him with his guns pointed steadily.

'Get up and let's have a look at you,' he ordered.

The horseman obeyed, picking up his sombrero from the dust. Oakes reached forward, took the horseman's guns from their holsters and stuck them in his own belt. Then he returned his own left gun to his hand.

'Vanquera,' he said, with a grim smile. 'I thought so! Rode right into it, didn't you?'

The outlaw did not answer, but his hard, swarthy face was bitter in the moonlight.

'You should know better than to fall for the gags of a law officer,' Oakes told him drily. 'I figure you were at the Lazy-G looking for fifty thousand in notes, huh? You're unlucky, Vanquera. There won't be that much money there at any time. I know all about it, and I'm running you in ... And keep your hands up!'

'You think you'll get me to law headquarters?' Vanquera sneered. 'With thirty miles of rough country to cross? Not on your tin-plate!'

'Get on your horse,' Oakes ordered.

Vanquera had to obey. He swung to the saddle. Using one gun to keep him covered Oakes retrieved his rifle and returned to his saddle; then he swung up and nudged his horse forward.

'Turn around,' he instructed. 'We're

going to Mowry City. They've got a jail there which will hold you while I attend to other business. On the way I'm picking up some of Mackenzie's boys to help me. I'm taking no thirty-mile trip with a sidewinder like you, my friend.'

His face grim, Vanquera swung his mount about and started forward with Oakes close behind him. They jogtrotted the distance to the Mackenzie spread within a few minutes; then Oakes fired twice into the air to attract atention. Within a few seconds half a dozen men, ready dressed, came tumbling out of the Lazy-G bunk-house and ran across the yard to the gates.

'Take it easy,' Oakes called. 'No shooting. I'm Jed Oakes, a Federal marshal. Right here I've an especial prize — Loupe Vanquera, in person.'

'Say, marshal, that's swell hearing!' Bart Moran, the Lazy-G's foreman, exclaimed. 'This critter's been wanted fur some time, so I hear. I figger you need help.'

Oakes descended from his horse,

puzzled for a moment.

'Say, don't any of you know what's been going on?' he demanded. 'About Mr Mackenzie, his daughter and the ransom money?'

'Huh?' Moran looked surprised in the moonlight, his men grouped around him. 'How come, marshal? Last time we heard of the boss he was joining Miss Flora and her party up at Skeleton Pass. Said he might be away some time. Something else been happening?'

Oakes gave him the facts as he had heard them from Mackenzie.

'Which accounts,' Oakes explained, 'for this jigger hanging around here, waiting for a chance to collect the money. I decoyed him out of hiding . . . What happened to Sheriff Friar who gave him the tip-off I don't know — but I've a pretty good notion.'

Vanquera looked about him as Oakes went on talking.

'You boys can take him over to Mowry City jail,' he continued. 'I'm going over to Skeleton Pass to . . .'

Suddenly Vanquera was off! One savage jab of the spurs was sufficient to hurtle his horse forward at the moment when Oakes, busy explaining, had forgotten to keep his gun levelled. Vanquera timed it perfectly. He swung his horse as it leapt under the impulse of the spurs, flinging its flying hoofs into the midst of the men, none of them mounted. Two were sent flying by the animal. Oakes whipped up his gun and dropped it as Vanquera's boot kicked him savagely across the side of the face. He dropped, blood brimming from a gaping cut, two of his teeth smashed out.

Bart Moran fired into the moonlight, but his aim was bad because of the plunging of Oakes's own startled horse. In a cloud of dust Vanquera thundered away, becoming a more difficult target with every second.

'After him!' Oakes gasped, his hand to his blood-smeared jaw. 'I can't make it right now. Got to get this cut fixed.'

Moran sprang on to the bucking

horse, grabbed the reins, then hurtled into the moonlight after the speck making good its escape. Oakes breathed hard, hand pressed to his aching face. Two of the men hurried away to the stables, brought out two more horses after a moment or two, then went speeding in the wake of their foreman.

'You'd better come in the bunk-house, marshal,' one of the remaining men said. 'You want that cut patching up.'

'I think you're right,' Oakes assented bitterly, and followed them across the yard.

In the bunk-house rough bandaging was sufficient to check the bleeding and a dose of brandy did the rest. Oakes began to feel more himself again and with it his fury rose.

'A lot of damned, confounded blockheads!' he snorted. 'I reckon that's what we are, letting him get away like that. I should have known never to relax — not with a louse like Vanquera anyways.'

He got to his feet, feeling several kinds of a pantywaist with the bandage wrapped about his face; then at the sound of hoofbeats in the yard he looked up expectantly. Presently Moran came in, his face grim, his two henchmen behind him.

'I reckon he ditched us, Mr Oakes,' he snapped.

'You *lost* him?' Oakes stared incredulously. 'But you just couldn't have in open country!'

'The dawn mist did it,' Moran answered. 'I don't have to tell you how it rises just before sunup. It's lying around outside thicker'n soup. We could hear that jigger for awhile — an' I reckon he could hear us — but we lost him. He got a blanket just when he needed it.'

Oakes swore; then he made up his mind.

'This makes things the devil of a lot worse,' he said. 'Now he knows there's no money coming his way he hasn't much reason to pull his punches in regard to Miss Flora and the rest of the party. The fact that I'm on to him will make him move extra fast. I've got to be after him right now . . . '

'We're with you,' Moran said. 'Boys, get the . . . '

'No, wait!' Oakes shook his head. 'It wouldn't do any good for all of us to go tearing off to Skeleton Pass: we'd make too good a target. I'm going, alone to begin with. Give me an hour's start and then follow just in case I've gotten myself tangled up somewheres.'

'OK,' Moran agreed promptly. 'How's about the jaw? You be all right?'

'Sure thing. Between the brandy and the bandage I'm a new man . . . Now I've got to move. Every moment's precious.'

6

In the one-time office adjoining the saloon in the ghost town of Hudson's Folly, Dick, Flora, Black Moon and Belinda were sitting with their backs to the wooden wall. Each one of them was securely bound, tightly enough to prevent them getting free, but not so tightly that cramp had developed. Up to now the only one who had suffered anything at all was Flora.

At regular intervals throughout the night the sadistic Shorty, following the orders left by Vanquera, had done his best to soften the girl up in the hopes that she would reveal the position of the gold. In fact Shorty had gone to the limit. He had ideas of his own. If he could locate the gold position before Vanquera returned he might do a good deal . . . but Flora had told nothing, because she could not.

Now she sat with her head drooping, the darkness masking the livid bruises on her face where she had been beaten up. On the backs of her hands and neck there were blisters where Shorty had indulged in fancywork with his smouldering cigarette. Flora was not unconscious, but she was utterly exhausted and all the fight had gone out of her.

'One hour and paleface return,' Black Moon said, after a while. 'We sit. Do nothing. White squaw suffer. Black Moon ache to destroy paleface.'

'Which means yuh protectin' Flora here?' Belinda asked. 'I don't get the angle, Black Moon. I thought all whites wus yuh nateral enemies?'

'Mister Dick a friend,' the redskin replied. 'White squaw Mackenzie his friend. Both friends of Black Moon.'

'You don't think I enjoy sitting around while Flora is tortured, do you?' Dick demanded. 'But how do we get out of it? We've no weapons — and we can't get free of these cords the cunning way they're tied.'

'Black Moon try,' the Indian said, as though an idea had struck him. Then there followed the sound of movement as he shifted his body. 'Mister Dick, turn your body to me,' he instructed.

Puzzled, Dick obeyed. After a moment or two he could feel the redskin's fingers — tied behind his back — tugging at the buckle of his pants belt. Then presently he had unfastened it.

'Now what?' Dick questioned.

'Cutting tool,' Black Moon explained. 'Buckle thin on edge. Fray cords.'

'That sure is one good idea,' Belinda commented, peering at the dim forms in the darkness. 'Can't figger why I didn't think of that meself. Mebbe because I don't wear a pants belt.'

For some time there was no sound as Black Moon worked steadily, scraping the edge of the buckle along the cord between his wrists. Meantime, as did Dick and Belinda, he kept his eyes on the closed door, expecting any minute that Shorty would return to continue his villainy. In the intervals, presumably, he got some sleep. Flora for her part remained exactly where she was seated on the floor, her senses dulled.

Black Moon gave a sudden ejaculation and with a wrench of his powerful arms he snapped the frayed cord holding him. To finish untying himself was only the work of a few moments, then he set to work to release the others.

'Now what?' Dick questioned, supporting Flora as she clung to him. 'We've no weapons . . .'

The redskin looked at the boards across the window. Through the chinks the stars were showing, somewhat pale as the dawn showed signs of approach.

'Planks well fastened,' he said. 'Much noise if we tried moving them. Wait for paleface to come again, then escape.'

'Only way,' Dick agreed. 'And you'd better take Flora, Belinda,' he added,

147

handing the girl over. 'I'll need my hands free.'

'So will I,' Belinda growled, holding Flora to her. 'Why can't yuh stand on yuh own two feet, gal?'

'I — I can try,' Flora whispered, and took hold of the wall to steady herself. Somehow she managed to remain upright though exhaustion and shock were still telling upon her, and the pain of her burns and bruises was by no means negligible.

'When that brute comes back in here he's my meat,' Dick murmured. 'That understood by everybody?'

Black Moon gripped Dick's arm in the darkness. 'Black Moon stronger in hands, Mister Dick. I will deal with paleface. You and white squaws escape, killing men in saloon. Can only be five of them.'

Dick did not like the idea even though he appreciated the wisdom of it, so finally he mumbled a grudging assent. Then it became a matter of waiting, watching the door with the glow of light beneath it from the saloon. Belinda moved over to Flora and put a strong arm about her waist to support her.

It was half an hour before anything happened, then there came the sound of footsteps across the boards of the saloon beyond. A shadow appeared at the bottom of the door.

Belinda released Flora and moved forward, her hands ready and her jaw tight. Dick retracted his forearm for a blow. Black Moon crouched like a coiled spring — then suddenly bethinking himself he darted back, picked up the ropes that had been binding him and the others, and tucked them loosely in the top of his trousers.

The door opened, and, half yawning, Shorty came into view, silhouetted by the glow of oil lamps beyond.

Black Moon sprang.

Out through the doorway went Dick and Belinda. Flora stood where she was, afraid to move in case in her giddiness she fell over. Black Moon had grasped Shorty before the gunman knew what had happened. Fingers of terrifying strength crushed into his neck and shut off the breath from his lungs.

He made a frantic effort to dislodge the hold, but against the redskin he stood no chance. He was forced down on to his knees, his head bursting. Only for a second did Black Moon release him and that was to whip one of the odd ropes from his waist and tighten it around Shorty's neck. Using a slip-knot Black Moon pulled tighter and tighter, then he secured the rope with a vicious twist.

Struggling desperately to free himself, Shorty kicked and lashed about the floor — but with every second air was dying within him and his strength failing. Finally, his face purple, he ceased struggling.

Not that Black Moon waited to see Shorty's end. The din from the saloon attracted him. He hurtled into it in time to see Dick struggling savagely with two of the gunmen, lashing out violently with his fists. The others were finding themselves hammered by the chair Belinda had picked up. With it whirling over her head she slammed down blows upon them which made it impossible for them to draw their guns. They had been asleep and the attack had caught them by surprise.

A fifth man was in a corner, his gun levelled. Instantly Black Moon leapt. The noise he made over it distracted the gunman for a moment — then he was flying backwards against the wall from a blinding uppercut. He had hardly hit the wall before another blow smashed across his nose. His gun vanished from his hand and pain exploded through his heart as Black Moon fired.

Dick staggered, missed his footing, and fell. Black Moon swung around from killing the fifth man and then his eyes gleamed. Swinging in the table-top only two feet away was his own treasured knife! He whipped it up and hurled it straight at the gunman who had Dick at his mercy. The vicious blade slashed across the man's wrist, baring it to the bone. He dropped his gun, the tendons severed, and before he could do anything further Dick was on his feet again and landed a haymaker which flung the badly wounded man across the old bar counter. He collapsed behind it and ceased to give any trouble.

'Plaster 'em, boys!' Belinda yelled, still whirling her chair on the hapless heads of the two men at her mercy. 'I ain't had such fun since Bluenose Calahan shot up a joint back in my home town . . .'

Dick dived, seized his remaining foe by the legs, and toppled him over his head. Three savage blows, one after the other, to the man's face and jaw, knocked the fight out of him. Black Moon jumped to his knife, whirled it up, then stuck it between his teeth. His next leap carried him to where Belinda was losing her chair battle to the two men trying to aim their guns between blows.

One of the men toppled backwards as the redskin landed on top of him. He made a frantic effort to bring round his gun butt to flay Black Moon across the skull, but instead the knife buried itself to the hilt in his jugular. Choking and gulping he collapsed helplessly, clawing at his neck.

Belinda jumped for her life as the last man aimed the gun at her. Up came Black Moon's foot and struck the gunman under his projecting chin. His teeth rattled and his gun flew out of his hand. Before he could do anything more the chair had whirled from Belinda for the last time. It crashed and broke on the man's skull, flattening him out.

'Which seems to be that,' Dick commented, wiping his streaming face with his sleeve. 'Nice work, Moony.'

The redskin put his knife back in the sheath in his belt. 'I get white squaw,' he said. 'We leave. Paleface outlaw soon return.'

He hurried into the adjoining office

and found Flora recovered enough to walk to the doorway.

'Black Moon carry,' he said briefly, and she found herself swept up into his powerful arms.

He followed Dick and Belinda across the saloon and out at the batwings. They looked up and down the empty street.

'OK,' Dick murmured. 'Nobody else to worry about. Better head out by the top end there. Far as I could gather the horses are in the old livery stable up there. We need 'em. Come on.'

He led the way down the street, Belinda beside him and the redskin carrying Flora in the rear — but before they had covered a dozen yards they suddenly beheld five men ahead of them stealing along in the shadows of the boardwalk.

'More of 'em!' Dick said abruptly, stopping. 'I thought we'd cleaned up the lot.'

What he did not know was that Sheriff Friar's men had been bunked lower down the street and had been aroused by the gunfire and noise from the saloon. Now, feeling that their lives depended on loyalty to Vanquera, they were on their way to investigate.

'In here!' Belinda said, and lunged for the building outside which she, Dick and Black Moon had stopped.

With her elbow she smashed the glass of the ancient door and scrambled through the frame. Dick followed her, taking Flora as Black Moon handed her in.

The five men were too far away at the moment to take aim, but the noise of the breaking glass gave them direction. They began running. Inside the building the quartet glanced around them hastily and in the dim moonlight could descry stacks of provisions and tinned foods — evidently the hideout's provender department.

'Behind those flour sacks,' Dick said quickly, and by the time the five gunmen had scrambled through the broken door the quartet had hidden itself behind a barrier of flour sacks, cans and wooden crates.

'I reckon they came in here,' one of the men said grimly.

'Yeah. Hey, wherever yuh are, come out an' show yuhselves! Yuh ain't gotta chance.'

'I'm not so sure he isn't right,' Dick muttered. 'Five of 'em, with two guns each from the look of it. Our only way out is here, at the back.'

He turned his head and peered into the gloom. A little to his left, leading between piled-up boxes, was an alley-way to a rear door. It offered prospect of escape, but certainly there would never be time to stop and look for horses.

'If we could get out we could dash for the foothills and figure the rest out afterwards,' Dick whispered. 'But if we shoot we give away our positions.'

'There's a better way than shootin',' Belinda murmured. 'Right now I've got me hand on a pile uv tinned stuff. I reckon that's all the ammunition we need t'confuse things while we git on our way. Moony, keep a hold on Flora so's y'can run with her. Dick an' me'll do the rest.'

The two men murmured agreement to her plan and Flora prepared herself to be suddenly borne away . . . Then Belinda acted. She felt for the nearest tin and flung it to a far corner of the store. As it hit the wall the men spun round and fired in that direction savagely; then they began a wild shooting affray as a hail of tins flew through the dim moonlight towards them. The tins were heavy, sharp-edged, and vicious assault weapons to heads and faces.

The men had a dim idea where the attack was coming from and fired blindly — chiefly into the barrier of flour sacks — but by this time Dick and Moony had darted down the narrow space between the cases, helping Flora along with them. Belinda stopped for a second longer to hurl a small crate. It broke over the head of the gunman who had caught sight of her and completely deflected his aim.

Then Belinda moved fast, through the deserted, dusty back regions and into the yard. Holding her skirt above her brawny knees she ran like the devil into the dawn light in the wake of the two men and the girl, and they kept on running until they had the rocks for cover and could afford to slow down a little.

At last they halted, breathing hard.

'Well, we got out,' Dick commented, 'but I don't quite know how much good it does us. We can't walk home, and there wasn't time to take any horses. And those guys will see that we don't in future. I just can't figure out who they are. I thought we'd taken care of them all.'

'Fact remains we're clear uv the bunch,' Belinda said, and spat emphatically. 'An' we ain't without chuck, neither. Take a look . . . '

From the bosom of her shirt she unloaded two meat tins, and from her shirt pockets two bottles of soft drink.

'Nice work,' Dick grinned.

'Sure is! Ain't no sense in bein' in a place full uv chuck an' doin' nothin' about it. And I reckon we'd better git somewheres *really* safe,' Belinda added, glancing at the lightening sky. 'Seems like dawn's goin' ter come like th' crack uv a whip an' we're goin' t'be seen mighty easy. Best git into them foothills and then start figgerin' what t'do next.'

Dick, carrying Flora in his arms, followed after her, and Black Moon came up in the rear. Before they had half completed their journey to the foothills the daylight came with its surprising suddenness, but even so they were not pursued. Evidently the men left behind knew better than to try and follow four fugitives in the tangled waste of rocks.

So, perhaps around eight in the morning, the quartet had reached the high rimrock overlooking Skeleton Pass and the site where they had been compelled to work. They were in fact on the remains of the ledge which had been the death of Pan Warlow and the cause of the landslide so many years before.

'Reckon this'll do,' Belinda said finally, as they came to a natural cup edged by rocky saw-teeth. 'We can be well hidden here but see what goes on below — if anythin' does.'

Tireless as usual she removed the cans from inside her shirt but it took Black Moon to open them. Using the hilt point of his hunting knife to drive a hole in the tins, he forced the tin slightly back by main strength, and from this small opening the contents had to be taken, piece by piece. At least it provided a meal of sorts and, washed down with the soft drinks, had some claims to being a breakfast.

'Without horses,' Flora said, looking and feeling a good deal better, 'I just don't see how we can ever get back home. It's a day's ride even on horseback. Trying to walk it without water or provisions we'd just wilt and die.'

'What *I* don't get is, what's happened to your father?' Dick asked, frowning. 'It's got me worried — especially since Vanquera is missing, too.'

Flora's expression changed and her dark eyes were suddenly alarmed.

'Great heavens, Dick, you don't think that perhaps . . . ?'

'I don't want to think anything, Flora, but I can't help noticing Vanquera's absence and your dad's non-appearance. Maybe Vanquera got wind of the fact that he's been around here, or something.'

'We not know; we not worry,' Black Moon said logically. 'We must get horses.'

He became silent again, gazing woodenly into the shimmering distances, his brain active. After a moment or two Belinda gave a sigh.

'I wish I knew just where that dad-blamed gold went,' she muttered. 'We spent all that time diggin' — an' look how fur down we got . . . ' She indicated the deep trough in the dusty pass below. 'But we didn't find a trace. Seems ter me that even if we didn't find th' gold we should ha' hit th' top uv the stagecoach.'

'It was probably smashed to matchwood and flattened out,' Flora said moodily. 'I get the idea that there just isn't any gold in that pass — that somebody took it away long ago.'

'If there's ever the chance we'll find out properly,' Dick declared. 'Ever occur to you that we never had an opportunity? We had blasting to do and all the stuff to do it, but things just sort of caught up on us.'

'When everything comes to be sorted out I'm to blame for what's happened,' Flora said seriously. 'I flew off the handle over what you said to me, Dick, and then I wandered off. I got captured and . . . Well, that was that!'

'It would have happened anyways,' Dick assured Flora and gave her slim shoulders a squeeze. 'Vanquera had tabs on us right from the start: things just happened sooner than we had expected, that's all.'

'Black Moon solve problem,' the redskin said. 'We not get four horses ourselves. Four horses come to us.'

'Just like that?' Dick asked.

'We wait till night,' Black Moon continued, unmoved. 'You fire shots near town. Attract men. Fire more shots from about here. Men follow. We ambush and take horses.'

'It's an idea,' Belinda reflected, rubbing the end of her snub nose.

'Suppose they don't use horses?' Flora asked, and Black Moon gave her a dour glance.

'When palefaces have horses they do not walk.'

'In the meantime we stay here?' Dick asked.

The redskin relaxed. 'We rest. Black Moon sleep. White squaw sleep too. You watch — with big squaw.'

'Good enough,' Dick agreed. 'Belinda and I keep on the look-out and Flora and you hit the hay . . . ' He glanced at Flora as she stretched herself out and pillowed her head on her arm. 'How's about those bruises and burns?' he asked.

'I'll get over them.' She gave a faint smile. 'No worse than the time when I was flung from a mustang into a branding fire.'

'I wish I'd been able to deal with that louse for what he did to you,' Dick muttered. Then he frowned. 'Incidentally, Moony, what *did* happen to him?'

'Paleface died.' The redskin had his eyes shut, his expressionless face to the sky. 'Rope choked him. Black Moon saw him dying. Black Moon well pleased.'

Dick compressed his lips and Flora, for all the hurt she had received, gave a little shudder. It was at moments like this when the difference between redskin and white became glaringly revealed. And, with the complete imperturbability of his race, Black Moon went to sleep.

So did Flora. It was towards two in the afternoon before she awakened, thoroughly refreshed. Another meal from the canned food and what remained of a soft drink, then Dick eyed the empty cans and bottles.

'Plenty of fresh water in the mountains,' he said, 'but food is another matter. We've got to get action as quickly as possible.'

'At nightfall,' Black Moon promised him. 'You sleep, Mister Dick, with big squaw. Black Moon watch, with little squaw . . . ' and he nodded to Flora who smiled slightly at the look of indignation on Belinda's florid features.

However, she seemed only too glad of the chance to relax and most certainly Dick was. They fell asleep almost immediately and awoke again to the night and a cool wind blowing down from the mountain heights.

'Anything doing?' Dick asked, stirring.

'No,' Black Moon answered. 'Black Moon wait for you and big squaw to wake. Black Moon go to fire gun.'

The redskin held out his hand to receive Dick's weapon, but Dick looked at him in surprise in the starlight.

'I thought you said I was going to do it?'

'Black Moon fast as the wind. Black Moon not get caught.'

'OK,' Dick agreed, and handed the gun over.

With hardly a sound the redskin vanished and there began for the remaining three another long wait. They did not hear the distant shots which the redskin must have fired. About an hour or more later he returned to the rimrock and fired twice over his head. The din was deafening in the confined area of the pass, the sound of the shots chattering back from the mountain faces.

'Men come,' Black Moon announced. 'They started when I fired near town. On horses. Hard for them to ride easy for Black Moon. These shots here will guide them . . .'

He paused, every muscle tensed as a hail of stones suddenly descended from the heights. It ceased almost immediately.

'The effect of your shooting,' Dick told him. 'This whole mountain face is in pretty dangerous condition. Remember the avalanche which buried the stagecoach.'

'Black Moon thought somebody above,' the Indian muttered.

Evidently he was wrong for no more stones fell. Dick took back his gun and then looked about him.

'What's the plan?' he asked.

'We go to floor of pass,' the redskin answered. 'There we wait. Soon men come.'

He motioned, and the three began to follow him down from the rimrock towards the rocks on a level with the pass floor. When they had reached it and taken to the rocks for cover Dick asked a question.

'We're armed. Do we shoot them down, or what?'

'We shoot,' Black Moon said, and listened intently for sounds of approaching hoof-beats.

'But I ain't gotta gun!' Belinda objected. 'I don't like it. I reckon I just don't feel th' same without me umbrella. Have ta use stones, that's all . . . ' And she looked around for, and found, two hefty chunks of rock which she held in readiness.

Evidently Black Moon's short cuts across the higher levels had only just given him enough time, for presently the sound of horsemen became quite distinct on the night air. Then as the hoof-beats came close five horsemen suddenly merged into view against the chalky whiteness of the pass floor.

'Right!' Dick said, and fired.

He missed his first objective, but the second time he succeeded. Black Moon, using Dick's second gun, fired too. Another man fell — but the remaining men opened up in retaliation, and having bandoliers of cartridges to draw upon they succeeded in keeping up the attack long after Black Moon and Dick had finished.

But they had forgotten Belinda. Standing up, and shielded by the darkness of the mountain face behind her, she whirled her right-hand rock with all the vigour of a baseball pitcher. It finally flew from her hand and struck the nearest horseman clean on the forehead. With a howl of pain he suddenly ceased firing, toppled from his saddle and crashed into the dust.

The two remaining horsemen increased their efforts, so Belinda tried again, and missed. Then Dick, Flora and Black Moon added their own stone contributions, hurling sharp-edged rocks with all their strength — but even so they did not have the accuracy of Belinda's first lucky shot, with the result that the horsemen came nearer and nearer, sniping as they did so.

'This isn't too healthy . . . ' Dick started to say, then he broke off at a sudden rumbling sound growing rapidly louder.

The gunman also stopped firing as they caught the ominous note in the still night air. The ground was commencing to tremble.

'An avalanche!' Flora gasped hoarsely. 'The noise of the shooting's done it . . . '

The gunmen had realized this at the same time. Whirling their horses round they raced hell-for-leather along the white dust of the pass, ignoring the three remaining horses and the riders who had been shot from them.

'We go!' Black Moon snapped out, as the din increased. 'Three horses there.'

He darted forward, stones already raining down with increasing force around him and the ground rumbling as though it were about to gulp inwards. Hard after him in the rising dust came Dick, clutching Flora, and Belinda with her divided skirt held up and her language violently unladylike.

A rock sailed three inches from her head and splintered on the spur she was passing. She increased her pace. Overhead, the growling grew to a roar as hundreds of tons of rock, dislodged from its perch by the sharp sound vibrations, got on the move.

By the time the quartet had reached the flour-like dust of the pass floor the avalanche was on its way down. Giant rocks and boulders were streaming down the mountain face against the stars, cascading, tumbling, cracking, hurtling outwards into space with a shattering din.

Black Moon reached the first horse and grabbed it. He swung round, seized Flora, and swung her up to the saddle. Then he leapt up behind her and lashed the frightened beast through the darkness and swirling dust. Belinda leapt to the saddle of the second horse, and Dick to the third. Scampering madly, the flood of rocks and spinning stones only a few yards from them, the horses raced out of the danger area and to the more protected regions of rock spurs beyond the pass floor itself.

Here, realizing they had escaped death only by a matter of a few seconds, the quartet drew rein and looked about them. The onslaught was all over now, its actual extent hazed in the choking clouds of dust: but as this began to clear it was evident that some four or five feet of rock had been added to the debris already in the pass. The bodies of the three slain gunmen had disappeared.

'Which puts us further off than ever from findin' that gold,' Belinda commented sourly. 'I reckon th' best thing we can do is head back to the Lazy-G as fast as we c'n go, even if we're dyin' uv starvation when we git there.'

'Best course,' Dick agreed. 'And before those remaining gunmen find us, too. We're unarmed, remember, as long as we have no bullets — and I don't think those owl-hooters can be far away.'

'Yore right,' a voice agreed, to the rear.

The quartet turned sharply from

looking at the pass. Not more than a few feet away, where formerly they had been hidden by rocks, were the two gunmen — and with them a third figure in a big sombrero tilted at an angle.

'Vanquera!' Dick ejaculated, and Flora gave a little gasp of horror as she realized what the return of the outlaw meant for her.

'Surprised?' Vanquera asked dryly. 'No reason why you should be. I was on my way back to Hudson's Folly along the mountain trail yonder when I heard all the shooting. I located it in time to see the avalanche and run into these men of mine. We saw what you were up to, so we just waited. Simply explained, I think.'

Dick felt his face grow hot with fury and frustration. That the whole desperate effort at escape had ended in again being brought face to face with the outlaw — and fully armed — was nearly too much for him.

'Get down from those horses,' Vanquera ordered, coming forward.

'You men take their weapons.'

Black Moon's hand ghosted down to his knife in the gloom, but Vanquera saw the action. His gun exploded and the redskin desisted as he felt the bullet miss the top of his head by a fraction.

'I'm not joking,' the outlaw snarled deliberately. 'Better hurry it up.'

The four descended to the dust and loose rockery, remaining passive as their weapons were removed.

'From what these men have been telling me, you've caused plenty of trouble while you've been on the loose,' Vanquera continued. 'A lot of my men badly injured; others killed. My storehouse partly depleted . . . I don't like that kind of thing and you're going to smart for it — and quickly. Once I've dealt with you I'm on my way 'cos I have the impression a marshal may come looking for me.'

'Not before it's time,' Dick commented.

'He won't be here yet. I got a long start on him . . . All right, start walking.

Y'know where Hudson's Folly is by this time.'

The quartet turned slowly and obeyed the order, the men bringing up the horses in the rear. Vanquera did not speak again until his saloon headquarters had been reached.

7

'Now,' he said deliberately, his dark eyes glinting in the lamplight, 'there's only one thing holding me back from killing all four of you right now — and that's the fact that I still believe you know where that gold's hidden. The avalanche has put it deeper down, I know, but I reckon you could still pin-point the place. Ted here tells me that Shorty got no information.'

Ted, the man who had had his wrist slashed by Black Moon's knife, was seated in a corner, his neckerchief tourniquetted round his arm. Near him were the bodies of the men who had been killed in the recent fracas.

'You're not a fool, Vanquera,' Dick said deliberately. 'Miss Mackenzie does not know where the gold is, any more than we do. Not the exact spot anyways. I told you that to begin with. If you want that yellow metal the only way is to dig up the whole pass, same as we'd have to do.'

'And expose myself to danger,' the outlaw said. 'That's the part I don't like . . . ' He thought for a while and then made his decision. 'OK, I think you're telling the truth — an' even if you're not I can't afford to waste time waiting for one of you to speak. I've a marshal hard after me. Only thing for me to do is to destroy this whole town, with all the evidence there is in it — and wipe out you four in the process so you can't talk.'

Vanquera motioned to the two gunmen beside him. 'Tie 'em up good,' he ordered. 'An' fasten 'em to the bar rail so's they can't roll their way out.'

The former followers of Sheriff Friar obeyed promptly, and within five minutes Dick, Flora, Black Moon and Belinda were all full-length on the floor, their ankles and wrists securely knotted to the old foot-rail at the base of the bar counter. Vanquera came over and studied them.

'Mebbe this is justice,' he said drily. 'You killed a lot of my men, so it can't be wrong if you get killed yourselves. OK, Ted,' he added to the man with the damaged wrist. 'Better come with me if you don't want to burn to death.'

'Burn!' Flora gasped, staring up in horror. 'Did you say — *burn?*'

'Yeah.' Vanquera grinned crookedly. 'Fire's an almighty powerful cleanser, they say: I might as well prove it. By the time this tinder-dry ghost town's burned to ashes there won't be a trace of you, or anything else. We'll see our friend the marshal scratching his head over that one. And don't think you'll fry quickly. I aim to drag it out. I'm starting the fire at the far end of the town and letting it catch up on you. That'll give you time to think about it.'

With that he jerked his head, and his three followers — the only ones remaining from the original band — accompanied him to the boardwalk outside. Vanquera looked about him as the ancient batwings swung shut.

'We start the fire under the chapel over there,' he said, pointing. 'With this south-easterly wind it will soon spread to the rest of the town and burn up the lot. I reckon it oughta act as a signal to the marshal who's after me. My idea is to do two things at once — kill off those four and attract the marshal, the only mug outside of Mackenzie who knows where I am. Mackenzie I can deal with later. We'll keep an eye open for the marshal from the rising ground clear of the town.'

The men nodded and glanced at one another in the starlight. Hard-baked barbarians though they were they had not the cruel inflexibility of purpose of the Mexican. Burning four people to death was a shade too much for their stomachs — but they could not argue and expect to live.

'I don't trust you gorillas,' Vanquera said, as though he had read their thoughts, 'so I'll light the fire myself.

You, Ted, get a couple of horses ready and turn the rest loose. We only want two: more would be difficult in a fire.'

Ted moved away to comply. Vanquera went down the steps to the street, continuing along it until he came to the extreme end where the ancient tabernacle stood. For him to gather straw shavings and odds and ends of stick and put them under the tabernacle itself — for it stood on props like the rest of the buildings — was only the work of a few moments; then he threw a lighted tallow into them and watched the flame commence to kindle brightly.

This done he got on the move and returned to where his men were waiting.

'OK,' he said curtly, swinging to the saddle. 'They'll never get free of that lot: it's spreading fast. Ted, you swing up behind me. You other mugs can ride that second horse. Now let's go.'

He set the animal moving swiftly down the main street and gave it no respite until the rising ground at the edge of the town had been reached. Here he halted and descended from the saddle. In a matter of moments his men were grouped around him, watching the flames already gaining a firm hold of the tabernacle and sending a cascade of sparks into the night air.

'Where do we go frum here, boss?' one of the men asked.

'Depends,' Vanquera muttered, his eyes on the spreading blaze. 'What's the worry?'

'I was thinkin' we've no foodstuffs. Ain't goin' t'be easy t'hold out.'

Vanquera turned, grinning a little. 'Take me for a mug, huh? I've got a dump outside the town full of tinned meat and bottled fizzwater. I put it there special in case of a run-out sometime. We'll get by.'

Satisfied, the men relaxed. To their slow-moving minds Vanquera was again reinstated as leader. He had the power of thinking ahead, and that was everything.

With a sudden crackling roar the

flames from the tabernacle leapt to the adjoining building, and immediately the bone-dry woodwork burst and expanded into further flame. In a matter of perhaps ten minutes the mass of the buildings around the saloon were alight: then the saloon itself was embraced in the holocaust. It went up like a torch, a skeleton of a building held up by its four walls with white heat inside it. The structure next to it began to smoke furiously and presently belched to a cloud of sparks which as quickly became flame.

'Sure is one nice bonfire,' one of the men commented. 'I can feel the heat frum here!'

'An' those four in the saloon musta found it kinda warm,' Vanquera commented. 'Guess they'll be fried to crisps by this time. Before long the whole town'll be — Take a look!' He broke off quickly.

With his men he gazed towards the further end of the main street. A lone horseman had just come into view, slowing his mount down as he looked about him. Vanquera's eyes glinted.

'It's him!' he breathed. 'It worked the way I figgered it. This blaze must look like a beacon in the sky . . . '

'Y'mean the marshal?' Ted demanded, tugging out his gun with his uninjured hand.

'Yes. I knew he wasn't far behind me . . . An' put your gun away. This is my party.'

Silently he stole away from his men, using the as yet unburned buildings on the opposite side of the main street for cover. By degrees he worked his way to where Jed Oakes — for it was he — was leaning on his saddle-horn, looking around him. A dark scar showed on his jaw and he looked exhausted from his long ride. And baffled, too. He had no idea if the four he was seeking were mixed up in the blaze or not. And Vanquera . . . ?

Oakes was soon to find out where he was. The outlaw's voice spoke from a few feet behind him.

'Get off your horse, Tin Badge, and make it quick!'

Oakes hipped round, his hand flying to his gun. Instantly Vanquera fired and the bullet scored a painful trough across Oakes's right shoulder. He held it tightly and slid from the saddle, his face grim and sweating in the blaze.

'I'm not going to kill you — yet,' Vanquera said. 'I prefer to see what happens to those I don't like, whenever I can. That's why I don't much like the thought of the four folks you're still looking for having died in the saloon yonder. I'll do better with you: I'll watch you die. As a marshal, the lowest form of skunk, I'm entitled to see you suffer plenty.'

'You mean you've trapped those four in *there*!' Oakes cried, gazing in horror at the collapsing roof of the saloon.

'Right! And I've some fancywork planned for you, too. I guess you walked right into my parlour, didn't you?'

Vanquera put his fingers to his mouth

and whistled shrilly. In response, his three followers presently appeared, trailing the horses beside them. Oakes merely glanced at them, then back to the fire which was now raging in all its fury along one side of the street. He still could not absorb the fact that the four he had been seeking were dead — as certainly they must be in such an all-consuming inferno.

'Get on your horse again,' Vanquera ordered. 'We're going places.'

Oakes found his guns taken from him, then, his shoulder paining him considerably and his shirt sticky with blood he climbed back into the saddle.

'Keep moving,' Vanquera told him; and Oakes found that the route took him away from the doomed ghost town and out towards the foothills and Skeleton Pass.

In the pass itself Vanquera did not stop. He still kept urging Oakes onwards along a rock trail, until finally they had arrived at a jutting promontory which projected like a gigantic stone dagger into space. Below was a sawtooth array of rocks.

'I reckon this might do,' Vanquera said, looking about him in the starlight. 'You gorillas keep an eye on this critter while I take a look above. There's something I want to be sure of.'

He nudged his horse sharply, goading it up to the heights. His men remained below and the only liberty they allowed Oakes was to let him bind his injured shoulder with his neckerchief. By the time he had done it Vanquera had returned. He dismounted and walked to the limit of the promontory, studying an upthrusting spur of rock, rising to perhaps eighteen feet. Then he considered the grey escarpment rearing to the stars.

'Do nicely,' he decided, and returned to his gathered men.

'What's the idea, boss?' one of them asked. 'You figgerin' on throwin' this guy in the canyon down there?'

'Nothing so ordinary,' the outlaw responded. 'I mean to make this jigger sweat. Any man connected with the Feds needs to die slowly — and then mebbe have himself found as a warning to others that it isn't always safe to hound a guy from state to state.'

'Anything you can figure out I can take,' Oakes snapped.

'Mebbe,' Vanquera responded enigmatically; then he took down a lariat from his saddle-horn and handed it to one of his men. 'Rope the guy to that rock spur at the end of the promontory.'

Oakes was seized, and with complete disregard for his injured shoulder, the men bundled him along the narrow ledge and forced him with his back to the rock. Since struggling was useless he had to submit, and within a few minutes he had been secured so tightly he could hardly move, his arms taut at his sides. He wondered vaguely what kind of scheme Vanquera had in mind.

'I reckon,' Ted said, 'that it would be quicker to drop him down there, boss.

He wouldn't stand a chance of living after it.'

'Too quick.' Vanquera came along the ledge and contemplated the taut ropes in the starlight. He tested them as Oakes eyed him bitterly; then finally he nodded. 'Do nicely. Now I'll tell you what I'm aiming to do, Mr Tin Badge. You'll find it unpleasant with your shoulder in that condition — but as far as I'm concerned the more unpleasant it is for you, the better. You can console yourself by thinking that at the first crack of dawn the end will come.'

Oakes did not reply. He was thinking of the men of the Lazy-G whom he had detailed to follow him an hour to the rear. He'd come fast: those men must surely be somewhere back on the trail — and they'd surely find him before dawn.

'What's th' dawn gotta do with it?' one of the gunmen demanded. 'Yuh don't expect this critter t'melt or fold up with sunstroke, do yuh? I guess marshals are tougher'n rock when it comes t'hardship.'

'He won't be tougher'n the rock that's coming down on him,' Vanquera answered drily. He jerked his head towards the mountain face. 'Up there, as I thought there would be after that landslide a while back, there's a lot of heavy boulders which didn't come down. They're only prevented from doing so by smaller stones blocking them, as a chock stops a wheel from turning. I've fixed those smaller stones in front of one particularly big boulder. They'll hold it back just as long as there's no wind — as there won't be in any strength during the night. But when the sun rises there's always a gale springs up in the mountain tops — and when that happens those stones'll dislodge. A boulder will come straight down that rough acclivity, along the promontory, and . . .'

The outlaw stopped, grinning in the dim light.

'Sort of pretty, isn't it?' he asked. 'Just like your boot might blot out an ant. Hope you enjoy thinking about it, Tin Badge,' he added. 'I'm going to settle somewheres where I can watch.'

Vanquera swung his horse and, his men beside him, led the way back along the narrow path and was presently lost to Oakes's view. He was left to work out his fate for himself — and it did not take much doing. When the dawn came the summit gales, brief but violent, would sign his death warrant — unless the men of the Lazy-G found him in time. He looked about him and listened anxiously, but there was no sound save the sighing of the night wind. Even the clattering hoofs in the stones from the horses of Vanquera and his followers had ceased.

And, if the boys of the Lazy-G did come upon this spot they would stand little chance. Vanquera had said he would watch from somewhere — anybody trying to affect a rescue would be little better than a clay pigeon. This thought made Oakes swear to himself and try desperately to move his shoulder to ease the pain in it. He failed and had to remain exactly as he was.

Meantime Vanquera was perched some fifty feet above the promontory. His men were around him. All resting their elbows on a protective rock ledge they looked down on the jutting finger where the dim figure of Oakes was bound. Finally Vanquera gave a chuckle.

'Pretty smart idea of mine, that,' he commented. 'Think we'll pitch camp here for the night, then be on our way.'

'To where?' Ted asked pointedly. 'Wherever it is we'd better get there quick. I want a sawbones to fix this wrist uv mine. I guess my hand's dead.'

'Like your head,' Vanquera said. 'And what the hell are you beefing about? The bleeding's stopped with that tourniquet fixed, hasn't it?'

'I guess so — but I need a doctor.'

'You can wait,' Vanquera decided. 'I've my own plans to work out first. If you got yourself cut you should be more careful. Keep an eye on that Tin Badge while I go back to the food dump for something to eat and drink. We're liable to be here some time so we may as well make ourselves comfortable.'

He nudged his horse and moved away from the ledge. His men looked after him. Ted spat significantly in the gloom and held his useless hand.

'Somethin' about that guy that plain stinks,' he said, ''specially when it comes to a kill-off. Always goes the long way round. I ain't so sure I like it. I'd rather rub a guy out at the end of a six-gun than make him wait fur it. I guess there's rules, even with jiggers yuh don't like.'

He looked down towards the solitary figure fastened to the rock.

'I think we're mugs,' one of Friar's men said, after reflection. 'There's still a chance of gettin' at that gold, but we can be purty sure that if Vanquera gets to it first we won't even get a smell uv it. So fur we ain't had the chance to deal with him, but we have now.'

The two other men turned their

heads slowly to look at him.

'Yuh mean shoot the coyote as he comes back?' Ted asked.

'Why not? He ain't no more important than a rattler in th' scheme uv things. When there's gold around I reckon the less there are t'share it, the better.'

The other two men said nothing, but their actions were sufficient. They took out their guns and propped the barrels on the rock ledge in front of them, their eyes fixed intently on the trail up which Vanquera would surely come on his return trip.

He was a long time. The distant red glow to the east which marked the funeral pyre of Hudson's Folly died out and the night became totally dark except for the stars — and still Vanquera showed no signs of coming back.

Presently Ted shifted uncomfortably and glanced around him.

'D'yuh suppose the guy's double-crossed us?' he asked. 'I guess he oughta be here by now. No sign of him anywheres on the trail . . . '

He got no further. A gun suddenly exploded from nearby and he sagged helplessly to the rocky ground.

'Same goes for you two yellow-bellies,' Vanquera snarled, firing savagely at the two remaining men before they could swing their cocked guns upon him. 'Try an' plug me as I came up the slope, huh? Lucky for me I came up the rear way 'cos it was nearer. Lucky I heard Ted say what he did. Luckier still I saw your hardware waiting for me . . . '

The two remaining men did not hear any more. The mortal wounds they had received had enveloped them in darkness. His face grim, Vanquera strode over to them and, one by one, he pitched them over the ledge and into space. Whether they were dead or not he did not know: certainly they would be after hitting the rocks below.

Oakes, cramped, his shoulder feeling as though it were on fire, saw the two bodies hurtle down, and wondered

— having heard the shots — what was transpiring above. In a way the incident cheered him. It would mean fewer men to deal with when — and if — the Lazy-G boys caught up.

Alone, and satisfied that he had cheated a double-cross, Vanquera settled down to the canned food and bottled drink which he had brought from his secret cache. When he had finished the meal he risked lighting one of his Mexican cheroots, keeping his hands well cupped round the tallow flame; then he moved to the rock ledge and leaned upon it, peering down at the hapless Oakes bound to the spur.

It was a faint sound in the night which made Vanquera suddenly look up. He crushed out his cheroot quickly and withdrew to the shadowy wall of the clearing. By degrees the sounds became louder, until at last a party of four men, picking their way and looking about them with guns at the ready, came into view. They had no horses and were following the back trail up which

Vanquera himself had come with his provisions.

He gave an anxious glance towards the two horses nearby, fearing at any moment that they would whinney. However, they were silent, half asleep, though their twitching ears against the stars showed that they were aware of alien sounds.

'I reckon the shootin' came from somewheres around here,' one of the men said at length, glancing about him.

Vanquera pressed himself further into the dense shadow and remained motionless. Evidently the newcomers did not see him for they remained beside the edge of the rock clearing looking about them. Then one of them suddenly pointed below.

'Say, take a look down there! Somebody hog-tied to a spur . . . Hey, down there! Are you gagged?'

'I'm Jed Oakes,' came a faint cry from the depths, and Vanquera's eyes glinted; but he did not act immediately. He watched the quartet move in a body to the declivity which led to the rock promontory below — then he went into action.

Sweeping the two lariats from the saddle-horn of the horse which had belonged to Ted, he made a gigantic noose and swung it gently in the starlight, waiting until the four men — of necessity close together — should pass immediately below him as they followed the zig-zag slope down to the promontory.

Presently they came in view. Vanquera tensed — then he threw the noose lightly but squarely, and immediately drew it tight. The men below were so surprised they did not realize what had happened until it was too late. Quickly the outlaw lashed the rope round the rock in front of him, then carried the free end to the saddle-horns of the two horses.

Savagely he belted them across the withers, then slipped away the rope loop on the rock. For a second it was slack and the men tried to escape its pinning grip — but immediately afterwards, as the two horses tried to escape Vanquera's blows upon them, the rope drew taut again, hauling the four savagely struggling men into the air.

When the horses had reached the mountain face they had perforce to stop, leaving the quartet swinging perhaps ten feet from the nearest stretch of ground, the rope cutting into their pinned arms. Two of the men still had their guns and they fired at the rope, but missed it. It was practically an impossible target in the darkness, with their upper arms pinned down.

Vanquera grinned and thought out what he should do next. To hold four men on the rope when he removed it from the horses was impossible, so he set the horses moving again, driving them around a nearby spur so that they took the rope with them, holding it taut meanwhile. Twice Vanquera made the horses perform their circus act — after which, with the rope ends cast loose, he was easily able to hold the rope with it twisted round the rocky pillar. He knotted it in position, then returned to survey the men as they dangled helplessly and swore.

'I don't know where you mugs blew in from, but you're not so smart,' he called down to them. 'If you want to know why I've tied you like that ask your pardner, Jed Oakes. The same boulder that's due to hit him at sunrise is due to hit you first. Be a nice, pleasant party I reckon.'

'What's the skunk talkin' about, Mr Oakes?' Bart Moran — the Lazy-G foreman — shouted.

Oakes explained — and Moran swore. He felt as if the rope was cutting an inch-thick gouge in his flesh. He dared not struggle too much to release himself for it made the situation worse, both for himself and his three comrades.

'No more men than you?' Oakes cried presently.

'I guess not, Mr Oakes. Makes it look as though Vanquera's got the drop on us — if it's Vanquera we're dealing with.'

'Nobody else would have the brains to think of this set-up,' the outlaw replied. 'If you'd have kept your eyes peeled you'd have seen two horses in the shadows up yonder. Fortunately for me, you didn't.'

With that he retired to his former position by the wall of the mountain, and relaxed. He lighted a fresh cheroot and drew on it placidly. There was nobody else could interfere with him now: Bart Moran had made that clear himself.

'Altogether, very nice,' Vanquera commented to himself, at the close of a long meditation. 'At dawn these guys get what's coming to them, then I can take the risk of looking around on my own for that gold. I've drawn the fangs of everybody who could have caused trouble, and that gold must be *somewheres* in that chasm if it takes me weeks to find it. I've enough provisions, two horses, plenty of ammo . . . ' He gave a complacent nod and enjoyed his cheroot all the more.

The only thing he did not like was that he could not afford to doze for a single instant, and in spite of himself he kept nodding at intervals, satiated by the food he had eaten and the mental balm of having disposed of his enemies. When he caught himself nodding for the third time he wondered if it really mattered if he slept. There was nobody left to worry him and he would awaken at dawn. The noise of the falling rock would see to that.

Deciding it was worth the gamble he went to the nodding horses and took the bedroll from the back of one of them. He fixed it on the ground and settled himself to slumber, ignoring the shouts for release from the four men who still hung helplessly in the grip of the taut rope.

As he had expected, Vanquera awoke at dawn. He stretched himself and glanced at the sky. It was grey with the rapid advance of sunlight. The ledge where he lay had become windy and it was the gritty dust in his face which had aroused him.

He rose stiffly and went to the rock ledge. The four men, practically unconscious from impeded circulation and the deadly cutting of the noose, still swung. Jed Oakes seemed to have completely lost his senses. His head was lolling, his arm and shoulder stained where blood had flowed.

Vanquera glanced above him at the dust swirling at the mountain heights. Before very long it would become the brief shrieking gale known as the dawn wind. And when that happened . . .

Vanquera gave a start. For a brief instant he caught a glimpse of a Stetson low down on the back trail. The owner of it was not looking up, but studying the ground at his feet.

'More of 'em!' Vanquera clenched his fists, the thought of his intended villainy being interrupted. The one thing he was living for was to witness the destruction of the men he had trapped.

He began moving stealthily until he had reached a point where he could look down on the back trail. In blank amazement he gazed upon Dick Crespin, who was wearing the Stetson, and with him were Black Moon, investigating the ground, Belinda, Flora — and a smaller figure in ragged clothes whom Vanquera did not immediately identify. Then out of his confusion it dawned on him. The smaller figure was the ragged young man who had dashed off into the unknown after being thrashed by Crazy Bill.

But why were the four adults not burned? They had been in the blazing saloon, and yet here they were — alive, apparently well, and coming ever nearer. Vanquera narrowed his eyes and drew his guns, sighting them carefully . . . and at the identical moment a grosbeak, carried by the wind, soared overhead with its wild, noisy squawking. Startled, the group below looked up — and saw Vanquera.

Instantly they moved, and his bullets

went wide of the mark; then they were out of his reach as far as the guns were concerned, concealed under the ledge immediately below him. Unarmed, it was the only course to take. Vanquera grinned, looked at the heights and the rising wind, and waited tensely for something to happen.

Under the ledge below the five looked at each other, Flora with her arm about the shoulders of the scared-looking young man.

'Well, what now?' Dick questioned, his face grim. 'You managed to track hoof-marks this far, Moony, and we know it's Vanquera up there — but how do we get him? He's armed, and we're not.'

'I don't figger what he's doin' up there,' Belinda said. 'Yuh'd have thought, if he had any sense, that he'd have gotten clear uv the state by now.'

'Perhaps somebody important is in his clutches,' Flora suggested. 'That marshal that he spoke of, maybe . . . '

'Black Moon has plan,' the Indian

said, looking around him. 'Dead vegetation under our feet. We light it. Great
smoke will rise.'

'So what?' Dick questioned.

'You will see.'

The redskin picked up a sliver of
stone and holding it like a rod between
his palms he spun it rapidly in the pile
of dry debris at his feet. After a moment
or two there was smoke, then finally
flame. Smoke gushed out quickly, and
went upwards.

'Keep fire smoking,' Black Moon
instructed. He pulled a clump of rock
lichen from the ledge wall behind him
and handed it over. 'This sappy,' he
explained. 'Make much smoke. Black
Moon deal with paleface outlaw!'

Dick, Flora and Belinda all nodded
promptly and searched around for all
the sappy vegetation they could find.
Black Moon watched until a dense
column of smoke was rolling upwards;
then he took a chance and plunged into
it. Keeping in its midst by moving in
the same direction as the still increasing

wind he climbed up the narrow face which separated him from the rimrock above.

Vanquera, for his part, was peering into the murk with his guns ready, alert for any trick which might be pulled.

Then suddenly he saw the redskin's crouching form through the smoke-wreaths. He swung his guns round to fire, but at the same time acrid clouds fumed around his eyes and set them smarting violently. He fired, but without any accuracy — then Black Moon had closed with him.

Vanquera struggled violently, on top of his form after the sleep he had had, but powerful though he was the redskin was far stronger. The outlaw gasped as a blow across the jaw dazed him for a moment — then his guns had been torn from his hands. He brought up his knees violently and planted them in the redskin's stomach. Black Moon gulped, lost his hold on Vanquera's neck, and fell backwards.

The outlaw dived for his guns, one in

the redskin's hand and the other in his belt — but instead of achieving his object he met a short-armed jab to the nose which set his head reeling with vivid stars.

Black Moon scrambled up, coughing in the dense smoke which whirled around him — and in those few seconds he lost sight of his quarry. Vanquera, in fact, divested of his weapons, was taking no more chances. He ran desperately, his footfalls receding into the distance as the smoke, billowing and swirling in the fast rising wind, hid him from sight.

The redskin turned impatiently and called below.

'Kill fire — and come up,' he shouted.

Dick yelled back an assent — and somebody else called as well. For a moment the redskin was puzzled; then as the cry came again he moved forward a few yards and looked over the edge of the narrow path where he stood. He saw Jed Oakes, tied to the pillar below, and the barely conscious men swinging from the rope. He saw the two passive horses also.

'Quick!' Oakes called weakly. 'A boulder — up there — coming down with the wind . . .'

Black Moon frowned, not quite understanding — then as he peered at the heights above he grasped the situation, his gaze fixed on a mighty boulder chocked in position by a small wall of little stones, the wind howling and shrieking around them.

Instantly he began moving, just as Dick, Flora, Belinda and the young man came up from the back trail.

'Cut white men free!' Black Moon said urgently. 'I have boulder to stop . . .'

He did not explain further but began to climb swiftly with his customary catlike agility. Half-way up the steep slope he paused, frozen in his tracks, the wind screaming around him. The small stones were moving, the sandy soil supporting them flowing away under wind action.

Two stones moved. The others began to shift gently under the massive weight of the boulder they were supporting.

'Look out!' Black Moon screamed — but to his horror the quartet was out of sight. The horses were there; the rope which had held the four men of the Lazy-G had been cut . . . Presumably the party was on the cliff end of the promontory.

Black Moon breathed hard, the wind shrieking a devil's wail about him. Then he saw the quartet moving to the far end of the promontory. They were cutting Oakes loose . . .

So much the redskin had time to see, then with a mighty roar the boulder moved. It rolled ponderously, gathering speed. He flattened himself against the slope, expecting the vast weight to blot the life out of him, but instead, the rock's momentum carried it forward into space. It bounced off an angle immediately above the Indian, shot into the air clean over him, and landed with a resounding impact further down the slope. Like a monstrous cannonball it followed the track Vanquera had expected, whizzed over the ledge below and out towards the promontory. It fell upon it with shattering force, breaking it off the cliff face like a carrot. With a series of dying rumbles the rockery collapsed into the chasm beyond.

Black Moon swallowed hard. So near a brush with death had left him shaken. How the others had fared he did not know: things had happened so swiftly. Possibly they had gone down with the promontory. Possibly . . .

He began to scramble back down the slope, reached the ledge below, and peered over it. For once his wooden face broke into a grin. Huddled against the cliff face below were four very much alive but frightened people, and around them five men lying on the narrow ledge which remained. They were stirring slowly, coming back to consciousness after the ordeal through which they had passed.

8

In a matter of a few minutes Black Moon had scrambled down to the ledge below. He found himself pumping Dick's hand.

'Black Moon thought you died,' he said anxiously.

'Pretty nearly did. Just saved this chap here,' Dick nodded to Oakes. 'Then the boulder came down. From the look of things Vanquera had a mighty nasty set-up planned.'

Jed Oakes stirred a little where he was lying. Flora looked up from the task of bandaging his wounded shoulder.

'No bullets to dig out,' she said. 'He got scored, that's all — but he's exhausted.'

'No wonder,' Belinda said. 'An' what about you men?'

She looked at the four from the

Lazy-G. Each of them was listless and cramped after the long period of rope-swinging they had undergone.

'I reckon Vanquera got the drop on us,' Bart Moran said. 'When I get my hands on that critter I'll . . . '

'Paleface outlaw gone,' Black Moon interrupted. 'Maybe lost. We go above,' he decided.

He went first up the difficult acclivity and helped the men after him. After perhaps fifteen minutes the entire party was safe on the higher ledge, the two restive horses which Vanquera had left pawing at the ground beneath them.

'Lucky you came when you did,' Jed Oakes said gratefully, holding his shoulder.

'I take it you're the law officer Vanquera mentioned?' Dick asked. 'How did you get on to us?'

Oakes told him — and Flora's face brightened.

'Then this means that my dad is safe?' she exclaimed. 'We got the idea that perhaps . . . '

'Safe and sound at my spread, Miss Mackenzie — or at least, he was when I last saw him, and I can't think of anything that can have happened to him since . . . But say,' he broke off, 'I can't figger out how you came to find me. Vanquera told me he'd locked you all up good and tight in that saloon and then set fire to it.'

'Sure he did,' Belinda responded, 'an' things were lookin' mighty tough fur us when in came this kid here . . . ' She nodded to the young man. 'Mighty brave he is, too. He risked certain death to git at us. He freed us just before the fire got to us.'

Jed Oakes looked at the ragged young man in puzzled silence. He was still frightened, it seemed, crouched against the cliff wall, his thin clothes hardly covering his bronzed, thin body.

'Any name, fella?' Oakes asked presently, and the unknown shook his head with its mass of rudely cut hair.

'He doesn't talk much,' Dick said. 'And when he does it's in a child-like sort of way. Brief sentences, I think he's had the living daylights scared out of him by Crazy Bill.'

'Who's he?' Oakes asked.

Flora took up the story and told of her rescuing the youth from Crazy Bill's whip.

'After which Vanquera shot Bill dead and had his body buried somewheres,' she finished. 'This young chap just darted off and we didn't see him again until he turned up fer the fire. From what he told us it seems he's always been keeping a watch on us. He wanted to repay me for saving him — and I don't think any repayment could have been more welcome.'

'Then what happened?' Oakes questioned.

'We were aiming for the foothills in the darkness,' Dick said. 'We heard horses overtaking us — we hadn't any, of course, and were moving on foot — so we hid ourselves and watched. We saw Vanquera, his men, and you, Mr Oakes. All of you being on horseback we lost sight of you mighty quickly. Things were obviously bad for you so Black Moon here started to trail you, following the horse tracks. It was an all-night job because some of the stony trails didn't leave any hoof-marks. Anyway, we finally picked up a lead, and the rest you know.'

'Mighty thankful you came when you did!' Oakes gave a heavy sigh. 'Vanquera certainly had things mapped out very nicely. You saw for yourselves what happened when the dawn wind blew that rock down.'

'And Vanquera's still on the loose,' Bart Moran said bitterly. 'That's the part I don't like.'

'No more than I do,' Oakes assured him, struggling to his feet. 'My job is to bring him in, dead or alive — and somehow I've got to do it. Right now, though, we've ourselves to think about. I must get my shoulder properly fixed, and you men need treatment for cuts where that rope held you. Above all things we need some food and drink. I suppose there must be mountain streams, but food's another matter.'

'I know where food is,' the young man said timidly, his scared eyes darting from one to the other, as though he expected to be hit at any moment. 'Vanquera has a lot hidden. I've seen him go to it. If you come I show you.'

'I'll come,' Dick answered. 'Being the least tired of any I can stand it. Vanquera can't do anything more since he's disarmed.'

He took one of the guns of the ranch boys for protection and then followed the young man from the ledge. Oakes watched him go.

'Have to take him to headquarters,' he said, 'and try and get him identified. He can't go on living wild, as he seems to have been doing.'

'Judging from what he told us he has a secret hideout somewheres in the mountains,' Flora remarked. 'He said we could go there and rest if we wanted. We'd be quite safe.'

'You might do worse. There are only two horses, and with such a big distance for them to cover across the desert they'll only be able to carry one rider apiece. So Dick and I had better go whilst the rest of you stay behind. Better tell the kid when he comes back that you'll be glad of his cave.'

The young man, however, was not satisfied with this when — with Dick — he returned with the tinned foods and bottled drinks from Vanquera's cache.

'Want all of you to see cave,' he insisted. 'Big secret there. Something you should see.'

The party, as they ate their meal, glanced at one another. Finally, after he had looked at the youth's face with its expression of eager anticipation, Dick gave a shrug.

'Better do as he says,' he suggested. 'If only to please him.'

So when the meal was over they followed the youth up a rocky trail — then up another one, all the time

217

ascending, until finally, at a point half-way to the summit of the lower mountain peaks, they came to a narrow trail perched along the edge of a dizzy canyon. Wearily the party looked about them, hoping there was something more than just a hole in the rocks at the end of the arduous struggle in the blazing sunlight. All of them had the feeling that the youth was slightly crazy, though the look on his face was not that of a half-wit. He actually seemed as though he were planning some tremendous surprise.

Finally, when he reached the solitary cave mouth, as lonely a hide-out as there could possibly be, with its commanding view of desert and pasture lands, he led the way into it. The party followed him, slowing down and halting, the view completely dark with the sudden transition from blinding sunshine.

Then, presently, when they could see again, they beheld the youth waiting for them at the back of the immense cave. He pointed excitedly to a pile of crates, and nearby to an assortment of objects ranging from an ancient pair of lamps to a rusty rifle.

'Treasures,' the young man explained, in delight. 'Now Uncle Bill's dead this is all mine. I have fun here.'

He went over to one of the ancient lamps to pick it up and hand it over, as a child might hand a valued toy to an indulgent adult — but Flora interrupted the proceedings.

'Look!' she gasped, pointing to the crates. 'Am I dreaming or . . . '

She hurried forward, scraping the grimed dirt from the crates' woodwork and then peering at stencilled letters. As they became clearer she looked with gleaming eyes, Dick, Belinda and the rest of the men astounded for the moment. The ragged young man was about the least concerned, holding an old lamp affectionately.

The crate lettering said simply:

MACKENZIE BANK.
MOWRY CITY

'Doggone it, it's the gold!' Belinda yelled. 'The cases frum the stagecoach that we've bin a-lookin' fur all this time . . . Bust 'em open!' she cried, nearly dancing with impatience.

To do this did not take above a few minutes, the ancient wood collapsing finally under hammer blows from pieces of rock. There lay revealed in the dim light the gold ingots which, so many years before, had been sent by Lanning Mackenzie on their way to Winslow, and had never got there.

'Pretty colour,' the young man said, gazing at the metal. 'I never knew what was in these cases.'

'From the look of things everything is here,' Dick said finally, after checking over the cases. 'What has me beaten is how it got here!'

'Uncle Bill made me carry cases,' the youth explained. 'I had to do it. He beat me if I didn't.'

It was perfectly clear the tremendous value of the gold made not the least impression on him. To him, the old lamp in his hand was far more precious.

'You mean you carried this stuff crate by crate from Skeleton Pass?' Flora asked, astonished.

The young man nodded and gave her a frightened glance.

'And what was Uncle Bill's idea in hiding the stuff here?' Dick demanded.

'He said he'd live proud one day. But instead he got crazier and crazier. He forgot these cases and lived in a hut in Hudson's Folly instead. He made me live with him, and work for him. I stole food from Buzzard's Bend. If I didn't do as he told me he beat me . . .'

Oakes turned thoughtfully from studying the ancient lamp in the youth's hand. It was obviously one from an old stagecoach.

'This,' Oakes said, 'and the one on the floor there, must have belonged to the coach destroyed in the landfall.'

'Yes,' the youth agreed promptly. 'Uncle Bill made me dig down until I found the coach. I knew where it was.

He made me drag out bodies and we buried them.'

'Just a minute, son,' Oakes said quietly, putting his hand on the youth's shoulder. 'You mean that you and Uncle Bill were on that coach to commence with, and therefore knew just where it was?'

'Yes. There was another man with Uncle Bill, and he got killed. And a woman inside. She was killed too. I — I think she was my mother, but somehow I don't quite know ... ' The youth pushed back the thick hair from his forehead. 'So many things happened to me when Uncle Bill thrashed me ... '

'Your Uncle Bill,' Oakes said deliberately, 'was actually Bill Himmel, the stagecoach driver. As fine a driver as ever there was — but evidently the shock of the accident unhinged his mind and he turned into a kind of crazy hermit. You escaped the disaster, too, but the shock upset your brain to such an extent that your memory became faulty as you grew older. Ill treatment didn't make things any the better for you, either. The woman, son, was your mother. She was the only woman on that coach . . . and she was my wife.'

For a moment there was silence, the youth staring in amazement at Oakes's craggy, tired face. Then Flora gave a little gasp.

'Then this — this is your son, Mr Oakes!' she exclaimed.

The marshal smiled. 'That's right.' His emotion was such that he had difficulty in speaking. 'For fifteen years I've fully believed that I lost both my wife and boy in that landfall, and now I find . . .'

He could not go any further. He drew the young man to him and put a powerful arm about the thin shoulders.

'I always knew I had a father somewhere,' the young man whispered. 'But Uncle Bill would never tell me anything. He even made me forget my name. Called me 'Loco'.'

'You're not loco, boy; you just didn't ever have a chance,' Oakes told him.

'But you will before you . . . '

At a sudden sound on the trail outside Oakes paused and looked up sharply. Dick and Black Moon turned and went to the cave mouth, looking about them. Apparently there was nothing unusual in sight — until a noose suddenly dropped from somewhere overhead and pinned their arms to their sides. Immediately they made a savage effort to free themselves, until rock crashed down on their heads with blinding force and knocked the senses out of them.

Puzzled by the mysterious commotion, the others turned from the back of the cave to investigate, and arrived in time to see Vanquera standing a few feet away, Dick's gun in his hand. Dick himself, and the Indian, lay unconscious at the outlaw's feet.

'Very touching story,' he said cynically. 'Fond pop reunited with sonny boy. And some good it's going to do you! Thanks for finding that gold: it's the one thing I've been waiting for . . .

Fine bunch of mugs you are,' he went on, advancing slowly. 'I've kept tabs on you ever since you left that ledge. All I had to do was pick up the rope you conveniently left behind and the rest was easy. I just had to entice these two critters outside' — he kicked Black Moon and Dick in the ribs — 'and deal with 'em. Could have been any two, just as long as I got a gun. Drop your hardware!' he commanded.

All save Bart Moran did as ordered. He tried to draw, and got a bullet clean in the chest as a reward. He gulped, clawed desperately at himself, and then toppled sideways. Before the others could do anything he had slid over the trail edge and vanished in the chasm beyond.

'That'll show you I'm not kidding,' Vanquera said. 'Not with two hundred thousand dollars in gold to play around with. Ever stop to think what a swell place you picked? Just a matter of two feet separating you from that chasm — and it's all of a hundred and fifty feet down.'

Reaching out with his foot he kicked the revolvers on the trail floor into the canyon beyond, reserving only one for his left hand. Then he grinned.

'Everything just as I like it,' he said. 'I can . . .'

'Yuh can what?' Belinda burst out angrily. 'D'yuh think yuh can deal with all uv us? Yuh must be loco . . .'

'Shut up, you,' Vanquera told her acidly. 'I never did like your face, or your manners. Mebbe you'd better be the first to go.'

'Go where?' she snapped, her red face nearly purple.

'Over this trail edge, of course: where'd you think? When I've gotten rid of the lot of you I can very soon rustle up some men to help carry this gold away. Go on, Ma, start walking. It'll be the shortest trip you ever made.'

Belinda hesitated, glancing at the edge of the pathway and the sheer drop beyond it. Then she set her jaw.

'Okay, if that's th' way yuh want it. I

ain't scared uv no side-winder with six-guns in his paws.'

Vanquera watched her narrowly as she moved to the trail edge.

'Belinda, no!' Flora cried hoarsely. 'Aunt . . .'

Belinda, however, had her own way of doing things. When she reached the trail edge she suddenly twisted round and flung herself flat at the same time. Out went her hands, seizing the surprised outlaw by the ankle. He fired, but Flora's upflung arm jolted his hand and the bullet sailed into space.

Belinda slipped, clinging to the rocky edge by her hands. Oakes dived, landing a tremendous right to Vanquera's jaw. In taking the risk she had, Belinda had given that split second which was needed to destroy Vanquera's advantage. He fired savagely and Flora gave a scream, reeling away with blood suddenly streaming down her face.

Startled, Jed Oakes turned to her, and received a smashing blow under the jaw. The remaining men of the Lazy-G darted forward, then stopped again as Vanquera got control of his guns and aimed them.

'Play games, huh?' he demanded, and brought down his boot-heel savagely on Belinda's fingers as she clung helplessly to the edge of the trail, her feet swinging in space.

'Yuh ornery no-account skunk!' she screamed at him, using only one hand to hold herself.

Vanquera grinned and prepared to bring down his boot on her other hand, which would certainly have dislodged her into the depths — but instead his ankle was seized as it rose and with tremendous violence he was pulled over on his face.

In his excitement he had forgotten that stunned men do not lie inert for ever. Dick, behind him, had recovered his senses and been quick to grasp the situation. Now he plunged on top of the outlaw as he swore savagely and fired his guns at random.

In another second his guns had gone: Jed Oakes saw to that. Then he returned to Flora as, her forehead bleeding freely from a vicious bullet slash, she half lay against the mountain-face, Oakes using her kerchief to stop the flow of blood. Dick, as he lay on top of the outlaw, saw exactly what had happened and it looked far worse than it was. Something took possession of him.

With all his strength he hauled up the battling outlaw and landed him a blow clean between the eyes. It slammed him hard against the cliff face. He used it to rebound himself, lashing up with his left. Dick absorbed it on the jaw and twirled giddily on the trail edge. It was Belinda, being helped up with a damaged hand by one of the men of the Lazy-G, who saved him. She cannoned into him and knocked him sideways, stopping his wild lurch. He swung, whipping up a haymaker that stopped Vanquera dead in his tracks as he plunged. His jaws seemed to click as they slammed together.

Safe on the inner side of the trail Dick went for the outlaw without mercy, working off all his hatred for the man in repayment for the injury he had caused Flora. In consequence Vanquera found himself pounded and battered right and left. Every time he aimed a blow it missed fire and was returned with interest, until finally he felt as if his head would explode with the concussions raining upon it.

In desperation he made a final wild lunge and slammed up his right with all his waning strength. It whizzed past Dick's ear as he jerked his head. In return he crashed out his left. It caught Vanquera off balance, at the end of his own smashing blow. He twirled, staggered helplessly, and tripped backwards. Before he could save himself he was putting one foot into the void . . . Then with a scream he was gone.

Dick hurled himself forward and was just in time to see the body, arms and legs flying helplessly, hurtling down to

the rocks a hundred and fifty
below. It landed — and remained s
  Dick rose up and hurried to the
of Flora. He looked anxiously at Oal
supporting the girl's shoulders, tl
back to the blood trickling from und
the bandage about the girl's forehead

'She'll be okay,' Oakes said. 'Only
flesh wound which stripped off the to
skin.'

Flora opened her eyes at that and
gave a faint smile.

'Nothing to worry over, Dick,' she
assured him. 'I've had worse than this
from horse kicks many a time.'

'Thank heaven!' Dick breathed. 'If
anything were to happen to you I think
I'd . . .'

He stopped, feeling curiously embarrassed with the faces turned towards
him. Getting up he went across to
where Black Moon was recovering and
helped him to his feet.

'There been fight?' he asked bitterly,
obviously furious with himself at having
been caught napping.

'Practically an earthquake,' Belinda told him, wrapping her damaged fingers in her kerchief. 'Vanquera took a nose dive inter the chasm here — an' best place fur him!'

She said no more. Instead, for some reason best known to herself, she began to study the rock near the spot where she had fallen over the edge.

'Which leaves nothing for it but to find a way home and get ourselves fixed,' Oakes said. 'We're minus poor Bart Moran, but I suppose we must write it down as just one of those things.'

'Black Moon ride for help,' the Indian said. 'Make repayment for being asleep while rest of you fought.'

The others smiled a little and Oakes put his arm about the ragged young man at his side.

'Mind leaving here, son?' he questioned.

The youth's expression was enough.

'Just one thing I want to know,' Flora said, sitting up and holding her bandaged forehead. 'What did you mean,

Dick, by stopping in mid-sentence when you referred to me? About anything happening to me, I mean. Not so very long ago you told me you didn't like the brazen way I proposed to you.'

He grinned. 'I didn't. That's why I nearly did it myself just now, only I thought mebbe you were too knocked about to listen.'

'No gal's too knocked about fur that,' Belinda said, lying flat on her face on the trail and peering around her. 'What the hell are you two kids waitin' fur? Dad-blame it, son, kiss her, can't yuh? Ain't the first time we've seen it happen.'

'First time with us it is,' Dick reminded her — but neither he nor Flora hesitated over the demonstration they gave.

'Seems like a wedding present might be in order,' Oakes commented. 'And I can think of a good one . . . The five thousand dollars offered for Vanquera, dead or alive.'

'Added to half the fortune in the

cave,' Dick said: then he looked in wonder at Belinda lying on her face. 'Belinda, what in heck are you doing?'

'I wus right!' Belinda yelled suddenly, leaping up — and she came over. Excitedly she extended her hand. In the calloused palm lay a small gold nugget.

'Where did that come from?' Flora asked breathlessly.

'I saw it when I fell over yonder ledge. I reckon it's rough gold — not frum one of them crates! Right around here there's gold fur the picking up. And when we've everything straight we're comin' back fur it . . . Yus, sir!'

She looked about her, and eagerly towards the sheer face of the mountains. She didn't know it, but she had located the bonanza which Pan Warlow had been blasting for fifteen years ago.